MYSTERY OF THE IVORY CHARM

What secret life-giving power does the exquisite ivory elephant charm contain? Can the trinket really protect its wearer from all harm?

Nancy Drew finds out when the owner of the Bengleton Wild-Animal Show asks her to investigate one of the performers who may be involved in some mysterious illegal scheme.

The girl detective's assignment becomes complicated when the elephant trainer's young assistant, Rishi, seeks refuge at the Drew home from his cruel foster father, Rai.

While following clues to help the boy find his real father, Nancy learns about an eerie abandoned house. She is harassed by its strange owner, Anita Allison, and the fiendish Rai.

How Nancy uses the ivory charm, reunites a maharaja with his son, and brings the evildoers to justice will mystify readers from beginning to end.

"Nancy, be careful," Bess warned fearfully.

Mystery
of the
Ivory Charm

BY CAROLYN KEENE

PUBLISHERS *Grosset & Dunlap* NEW YORK

Contents

Mystery
of the
Ivory Charm

CHAPTER I

An Angry Elephant

NANCY sat in her father's law office, waiting for him to finish a long-distance call.

As he cradled the telephone, she said, "What's up, Dad? Another mystery?"

Mr. Drew nodded and smiled. "It concerns a member of a wild-animal show."

"Man or beast?" his eighteen-year-old daughter teased, her blue eyes twinkling.

"Maybe both," the tall, handsome lawyer replied. "That's for you to find out."

He explained that his friend, Mr. Stanley Strong, who owned the traveling Bengleton Wild-Animal Show, had asked to consult him about some suspicious and perhaps illegal proceedings.

"There will be a performance tomorrow afternoon in Tannberg," Mr. Drew went on. "Unfortunately, I can't go, and Mr. Strong said he preferred not to discuss the case over the phone. So I thought I'd send you.

"After the show he'll be glad to tell you about his suspicions. He sent me four front-row seats," Mr. Drew added, pulling the tickets out of his pocket. "Can you make it?"

"Indeed I can," Nancy replied. "I'll ask Bess and George to come." Bess Marvin and George Fayne were girl cousins who often helped Nancy. "And I can take little Tommy from down the street. He'll love the special elephant act from India I saw advertised."

"Don't let him get into any mischief," her father warned, knowing the boy's tendencies.

Nancy laughed. "I promise." She took the tickets and rose to leave.

"Good luck," the lawyer said.

His slender, attractive daughter walked toward the car. It was a sunny, warm May afternoon. Nancy's strawberry-blond hair vividly contrasted her teal-blue convertible.

As soon as she reached home, Nancy phoned Bess and George, who were eager to attend the wild-animal show. Tommy was also ecstatic over the idea. He came up to the Drew house at once to show his delight by doing a series of somersaults, cartwheels, and Indian war whoops.

"We're going to have a super time," the five-year-old blond-haired boy predicted.

The following afternoon Tommy was on hand

promptly, and he set off with Nancy, first to pick up pretty, blond, and slightly overweight Bess, then boyish, dark-haired George.

"I hope we see elephants," said Tommy as the car neared Tannberg half an hour later. "Someday I want to ride one."

Nancy smiled. "There'll be a special elephant act."

As she drew closer to the fairgrounds, the group began to feel the festive atmosphere. People were hurrying toward the entrance, flags were flying, and a brass band was playing.

Nancy found a parking space. "Would you like to go directly to our seats, or shall we look around first?" she asked her friends as they walked toward the grounds.

"Let's find the animal cages first," Bess suggested.

She and the others had just reached the area, when Tommy spied a vendor who was selling fresh-roasted peanuts.

"Oh, Nancy, please buy me a bag so I can feed them to the elephants."

Bess offered to do it and added, "I'd like to give some to the monkeys."

Her cousin George spoke up. "I understand it's against the rules to feed the monkeys. I guess in the jungle it's all right for them to eat the nuts raw, but here ours are too well——"

She never finished the sentence because at this

moment the crowd nearby began to scatter. A huge elephant was slowly plodding down the passageway toward them.

"Run!" cried Bess, scooting out of the way.

Nancy held Tommy's hand tightly. She noticed a handsome, olive-skinned boy of about twelve years, wearing a bright-green tunic over straight-legged white pants, hurrying after the beast. Some distance behind him was a tall slender man, dressed in a long exotic-looking gown and turban. He carried a whip and a metal-tipped stick.

George was fascinated but said, "I hope that man doesn't intend to use those things on the elephant. It will certainly get mad and might trample anyone in its path. In any case, it'll begin to trumpet."

"Trumpet?" Tommy questioned. "Where does an elephant carry a trumpet?"

The girls smiled. Nancy explained to the little boy that when elephants become angry, they swing their trunks around in the air and sometimes make loud sounds that slightly resemble those of a trumpet.

Tommy thought the explanation was funny. Just as the elephant stomped by them, it raised its trunk a bit as if sniffing the air.

Suddenly Tommy jerked away from Nancy and ran to the great beast. With surprising agility, the little boy swung his arms and one leg up onto the elephant's trunk.

"Oh!" Bess exclaimed.

Several people in the crowd screamed. It was Nancy, however, who rushed to Tommy's aid. By this time the annoyed elephant was trying to fling the boy off. Tommy clung tightly but looked terrified.

"I'll catch you," Nancy offered.

He released his hold and fell into Nancy's outstretched arms. His weight caused her to stumble backward.

When she set Tommy on his feet, he began to cry. The elephant had stopped walking and now turned his head toward Nancy and Tommy. Did he intend to attack them both?

By this time a boy who looked like a native of India had rushed up. He stood alongside the elephant and spoke softly to him in words his listeners did not understand.

"Shānt ho jao dost!" Rishi said. ("Be calm, friend!")

"I guess," said George, "he's talking Hindi."

Just then the man who had been running after the boy and the elephant dashed up. He spoke angrily to them and flourished the whip but did not strike either the boy or the beast. The young helper cringed, however.

The man now turned his attention to Nancy and Tommy. In English he said sharply, "Why don't you watch your boy better? He's a nuisance. You should take him home at once."

Nancy eyed the man steadfastly, then said, "I'm sure Tommy regrets what he has done. But since he didn't harm the elephant or any of the people here, I see no reason why he shouldn't stay. I'm sure he'll behave."

The animal trainer said no more to her but again turned to the boy. In English he shouted, "Rishi, you will be punished for this! Your job is to guard old Arun, and you let him get away!" Once more he brandished the whip.

Nancy sprang forward. "Don't touch that boy!" she cried out.

The man looked at her with scorn. "I am Rai, the great Rai. This is my son. I can whip him if I want to."

"Not in America," Nancy said firmly.

The man laughed raucously. "I am not subject to the laws of your country. We are from India."

What might have become a very ugly scene was interrupted by the arrival of Rai's assistant and two guards. The situation was quickly explained to them.

One guard said, "Rai, you'd better talk the matter over with Mr. Strong. Right now I'd advise you to go back to your quarters and wait for the show."

Rai looked at the man angrily but said nothing. Rishi led the animal from the crowded area. Nancy and her friends hurried away. Tommy,

"I'll catch you," Nancy offered.

still shaking from fright, promised he would behave.

Bess winked at George and Nancy as if to say,
"Well, at least for a while!"

As they wandered along, Bess stopped at a
booth where stuffed wild animals were being sold.
"Look at this darling panda," she said, picking up
one of the plush black-and-white-haired animals.
"I'm going to buy him."

At this moment Nancy realized that someone
was standing beside her and she turned to see
Rishi.

"Hello!" he said shyly. "Rishi not speak English much. Thank you for help me."

"I was glad to do it," she said. "Tell me about
yourself. Do you travel with the wild-animal show
all the time?"

"Yes. Rai makes me."

George spoke. "Don't you go to school?"

"No school," Rishi answered. "Man in circus
teach me."

As the group turned toward the big tent where
the show would be held, Bess said, "Nancy, I don't
want to carry this panda around. Suppose I put
it in the trunk of your car. May I have your key?"

Nancy opened her purse and handed Bess the
key case. As Bess turned toward the parking area,
Tommy said, "I want to go with you."

She took his hand, and the two went off. Rishi
followed them and Nancy did not stop him.

A moment later Nancy was glad she had not. Rai was coming back! He stopped in front of Nancy and George. "Where is my son, Rishi?" he demanded.

The girls preferred not to tell the cruel-faced man what they knew. Instead they looked around and George said, "I don't see him."

Nancy's eyes became fastened on an unusual, beautiful carved-ivory elephant charm that the man wore on a black velvet cord around his neck. She mentioned it to him.

"It is very old and very rare," Rai replied, still with a trace of annoyance in his voice. "Besides, the charm has special meaning. The person who wears it is protected from harm. I wear it when I am around the elephants. Sometimes one of them becomes ugly."

The man strode off. In a few minutes Bess and Tommy returned, but Rishi was not with them. They said he had gone to prepare for the performance.

"Let's go inside," Tommy urged.

The show was even better than the advertisements had promised. The lion acts, the tigers, and the dancing elephants were enthusiastically applauded.

"Here comes Rishi!" exclaimed Bess, as he made his entrance.

The young Hindu boy sat astride old Arun's trunk. Little by little the lad climbed to the tip of it. With a sudden flip, the elephant threw Rishi into the air. The boy neatly executed a somersault and landed on Arun's back while the animal continued his steady rhythmic plodding around the ring.

Every few minutes Rishi would repeat his performance to the delight and amazement of the crowd. Everyone clapped loudly and Tommy was on his feet, waving both arms and screaming, "Do it again! Do it again!"

When the whole show was over, everyone agreed that the little acrobat from India was the best performer. Over and over he was called to take final bows. His father, Rai, stood in the background, looking very unhappy.

"He should be proud of his son," George remarked. "Instead he acts as if he'd eaten a box of tacks."

Bess giggled. "Maybe he's jealous."

Nancy and her friends hurried to Mr. Strong's trailer-office. Bess and George offered to keep Tommy busy outside while Nancy had her conference.

"Come in!" the owner of the wild-animal show greeted Nancy. He smiled broadly. "Your father has great faith in your ability to solve mysteries. Well, here's a sticky one for you."

He went on to say that the man in charge of the elephants, named Rai, was a strange person. "He's very secretive and thinks it is perfectly all right to disobey United States laws because he's an alien. I haven't caught him in anything illegal, but I've told him many times that if he does not change this attitude, he will certainly get into trouble with the authorities.

"Rai feels that how he treats Rishi is his own business. Once I threatened to report him. Afterward, his behavior toward Rishi seemed to improve. But it didn't last long."

Nancy nodded. "We saw evidence of that before the show began."

The owner continued, "Several times I've thought of discharging Rai, but I haven't done it because I'm very fond of Rishi."

Mr. Strong said that he wanted the Drews to find out more about Rai and his background. "He apparently is in this country with proper credentials, but I feel that there's something sinister behind the whole thing."

"Can you give me any ideas?" Nancy questioned.

"I'm afraid not," Mr. Strong replied. "But I'm sure it will not be long before you have some."

"We'll do our best," Nancy promised.

She met Bess, George, and Tommy outside. They went to the car immediately. Many people had already gone, leaving the parking lot almost empty.

When the group reached Nancy's house, she suggested that everyone come in and have a refreshing drink. Before anybody could accept, they were startled to hear loud banging from inside the car trunk.

Nancy hurried to the back of the vehicle and unlocked the lid. As it sprang up, a boy began to climb out!

"Rishi!" Nancy exclaimed.

CHAPTER II

A Doubtful Gift

THE group stared at Rishi. Finally Nancy said, "How did you get into the trunk?"

There was silence for a few seconds; then Rishi and Tommy looked at each other. Finally Tommy revealed that he had not closed the car's trunk lid securely.

"I wanted the panda to have some air," he explained, "so I asked Bess to let me shut the lid." The little boy grinned. "But I didn't close it tight."

Rishi spoke up. "Rishi see chance run away from Rai. Rishi tell you more."

Nancy interrupted him and suggested that Tommy had better run home. "I'm sure your mother will be looking for you."

Tommy skipped off. Nancy invited all three into the house, saying to Rishi, "Then you can tell us your story."

Nancy went to get some cool drinks before the strange tale began. After Hannah was introduced to the Hindu boy, she took him off so he could tidy up his appearance. When he returned, Rishi looked even more handsome than he had before.

"Rishi have two mothers in India. One wife to Rai. She nice to me. One day take Rishi to park. Big house. Mother say, 'Rishi should live here, not with animals!' "

His listeners nodded but said nothing.

"Mother become very sick. Tell secret to Rishi. Must never tell Rai. Mother say she not Rishi's real mother but get him when baby. Rai not real father. Real mother dead, and real father in America in River Heights."

The boy gulped back tears, then went on, "Tell Rishi if animal show bring him near here sometime, look for real father. She say, 'Rishi tell him *Manohar.*' Real father will know what word mean. He think Rishi dead. He will know truth when Rishi say *Manohar.*"

Nancy and the other girls were excited by this information. Nancy asked the boy what his real father's name and address were. Rishi merely shrugged.

"Rai's wife die before she tell Rishi."

The three girls knew that this assignment would be difficult. The man who was supposed to be Rishi's real father might have moved away from River Heights, or he might have returned to India. He could even have died!

Nancy rose and said she would go to the police and try to get some information. Noticing Rishi's frightened look, she said, "Don't worry. Nothing is going to happen to you, Rishi. I'll make sure of that."

Fortunately, Nancy's friend Chief McGinnis was at his desk when she arrived, so she was able to talk to him privately. She related Rishi's story and asked if the chief knew of any man from India who was living in River Heights.

"Yes, I do," McGinnis replied. "His name is Vivek Tilak and he lives in a large house out on Bradford Avenue. He's an importer and a fine gentleman. Be sure to let me know what you find out, Nancy. This is an intriguing situation."

Nancy promised to do so and obtained the number of the Tilak house. When she returned home and entered the living room, Nancy smiled at Rishi and said, "We have one very good lead. Let's follow it."

Next she asked the boy if he had any idea what the word *Manohar* meant. He shook his head and replied, "Rishi never hear it, except one time."

The boy and his new-found friends were excited as they climbed into Nancy's car and went to Bradford Avenue. When they reached the attractive Tilak residence, the four walked up to the front door together. Nancy suggested that Rishi ring the bell.

Everyone waited anxiously to see who would answer. To their disappointment no one came to the door. They tried the bell again, letting it ring a long time. No one appeared. Rishi suddenly put his arms around Nancy and trembled a little. She patted him soothingly.

"I know this is hard for you, dear, but we won't give up. Mr. Tilak is probably at work. Let's find out if any of his neighbors know where he is."

Bess and George returned to the car, while Nancy and Rishi walked to the next house. Again there was no answer. They hurried across the street and rang the bell of another neighbor's home.

This time a woman appeared at the door. She smiled at them. "Yes?"

Nancy explained that they were trying to get in touch with Mr. Tilak. "Could you tell me where we can find him?"

"Yes," she answered. "When he is in the United States, he spends most of his time at home, but he travels a great deal. Mr. Tilak goes back and forth to India a lot. He's there right now."

Again Rishi's enthusiasm and smile had turned to a look of sadness. This was not lost on Mr. Tilak's neighbor.

"I understand he'll return in three weeks," she

said. "Why don't you leave a note for him to get in touch with you at that time?"

"We'll come again," Nancy told her. "Thank you very much for the information. This boy is from India and is eager to see him." Rishi smiled shyly.

"I understand," the neighbor said. "Mr. Tilak is a charming gentleman. I know little about his life, but I believe a good part of it was sad. Now he keeps very busy and that takes his mind off the past."

Nancy thanked her and left with Rishi.

"Any luck?" George asked as the two got into the car.

"Yes and no," Nancy replied and then told them what she had learned. She dropped Bess and George at their homes and went on. During the drive she kept wondering what her next move should be and finally decided to phone her father to ask his advice. As soon as she reached her own home, Nancy called his office.

The lawyer was astounded at the progress Nancy had already made, but said Rishi must be returned to Rai at the wild-animal show. Whether or not the man was the boy's real father had nothing to do with it. For the time being, Rai claimed that Rishi was his son and he had taken care of the boy since his infancy. Nancy's heart sank at the thought of sending Rishi back.

When Nancy explained this to Rishi he tried hard not to cry. "Rishi so happy for little while," he said. "Now bad news come."

He pleaded with the girl to let him stay at her house. In his halting English he told her about Rai's cruelty to him—relating incidents about which Mr. Strong, the owner of the show, knew nothing.

"I'll tell you what I'll do," Nancy said. "Instead of taking you back to the show, I'll phone Mr. Strong to let him know you're safe. Then I'll ask him what he thinks we should do."

In order to avoid upsetting the boy Nancy went upstairs to phone while Hannah took Rishi to the kitchen and tried to interest him in dinner preparations.

Meanwhile, Nancy had dialed the number of the show and in a few seconds was talking with Mr. Strong. He was astonished to hear where Rishi was and how he had managed to get there.

"I assumed he had gone off with Rai. This will surprise you, but Rai suddenly resigned and told his assistant he was leaving and would not come back."

Nancy was astounded by this turn of events. Had Rai deliberately abandoned Rishi because he had learned of Strong's suspicions about him, or had he left the animal show to hunt for Rishi? She asked Mr. Strong what he thought.

The show owner was perplexed. "One thing I

certainly know," he said, "is that Rishi is much better off with you than he would be here. Until Rai returns, would you be willing to keep Rishi at your house? I suppose I'm now his guardian, and I'd like him to be with you until we learn more about Rai. I'm sure Rai would have no idea Rishi is there, so he can't come and make trouble."

Secretly Nancy was pleased by the suggestion. She said she would have to consult her father and Hannah Gruen before saying yes.

"I'll call you right back, Mr. Strong," she said.

Mr. Drew and Hannah agreed to the plan but said Nancy should warn the boy not to go anywhere.

"He must stay in the house or right on our property," the lawyer declared.

When Nancy spoke to Mr. Strong again, he seemed relieved by the arrangements. "If I hear from Rai, I'll call you at once," he promised.

"And I will let you know if we learn anything from or about him, or Mr. Tilak," Nancy told the show owner.

Nancy hurried downstairs and went directly to the kitchen. She put her arms around Rishi and gave him a little hug. "Everything is all right," she said. "You are to stay with us for now. But remember to be careful. Remain in the house most of the time and when you do go outdoors, watch out."

For the next hour Nancy and Rishi could talk of nothing but his good fortune. He wanted to know what work he could do around the house.

"Rishi always do hard work," he said.

Hannah Gruen laughed. "So glad to hear that, because I could use a little extra assistance around here. I'll let you know tomorrow how you can help me."

Mr. Drew came home early and at once became friendly with Rishi. He took him on a short tour of the house to show the boy mementos he had collected from various places in the world. Rishi was intrigued.

He said, "Mr. Drew have souvenir from India?"

"Only one small rug," the lawyer replied.

"Rishi get you more things," the boy promised.

During dinner the young visitor became very quiet and picked at his food. Hannah was afraid he did not like her cooking, but Nancy and her father thought the boy's loss of appetite was a reaction to his exciting day.

They talked of many things and he answered politely. He offered no conversation, though, until after dessert had been served.

Then, from a pocket, he pulled the beautiful ivory elephant charm that Rai had worn. After getting up from his chair, he walked over to Nancy and put it around her neck.

"This for you to keep," he said, making a low bow.

Nancy was overwhelmed. "But this belongs to Rai! How did you get it?"

Rishi explained that he saw it lying on the table in Rai's quarters after the show. "Rishi pick up charm and put in pocket. Nancy must have this," he insisted. "She very good girl and help me find my true father."

CHAPTER III

Missing Guest

EVERYONE at the table stared at the beautiful elephant ivory charm.

"This is exquisite!" Nancy looked at Rishi, wondering how to explain that she could not accept such a gift. Finally she said, "Rishi, dear, you are most thoughtful to want me to have this. You say Rai had laid it on a table and gone off without wearing it?"

The boy told her that in a fit of temper Rai had yanked the charm from his neck and thrown it on the table, saying he never wanted to see it again.

"Rishi pick up. Rai always say wearer have good luck."

"I recall Rai saying that," Nancy replied. She was puzzled. "Why would he have stopped wearing it?" she asked. Smiling, she added, "How strange for anyone to deliberately throw away good luck!"

Rishi shrugged and said Nancy did not understand the man. "Rishi pick up elephant charm and bring here. Nancy keep it. Have good luck."

The young sleuth sighed. "I certainly hope to have good luck in finding your father, Rishi. But the charm must be given back to its owner if he wants it. As soon as we hear of Rai's return, I will see that he learns about it. In the meantime, though, I'd love to wear the charm."

Rishi beamed. "Rishi hope Rai never come back."

Mr. Drew changed the subject. "What is Mr. Strong going to do without the elephant act and your special performance?"

When Rishi did not reply, Nancy said, "I must tell you exactly what Rishi is able to do. It is very difficult." She described his act to her father.

Rishi, who was still standing, put his chin up and threw back his head. He was so erect and had such a regal bearing that the others were convinced that a man like the cruel, dictatorial Rai could not be his real father. Nancy even wondered if the animal trainer might have stolen the charm.

Her thoughts were brought back to Rishi, who remarked wistfully, "Rishi not miss Rai, but miss Arun very much."

The Indian boy went on to say that sometimes
he hid from Rai to avoid being punished for
some deed he had not committed. The man had
a suspicious nature. He avoided making friends
with anyone connected with the show and acted
as though he thought someone was after him.

"When Rishi hide," the boy said, "sleep with
old Arun. Elephant very warm and Rishi trust
him." Little by little the boy's listeners felt more
sorry about his situation and became more fond
of him. Each wanted to do everything he could
to help Rishi lead a happier life.

As everyone left the table, he said, "Rishi go to
bed now. Get up four o'clock."

The others gasped and Hannah Gruen said,
"Four o'clock! Not in this house. You may sleep
until seven o'clock."

Rishi insisted he wanted to go to bed, and the
others realized that if he had been up since four
o'clock that morning, he must indeed be very
tired. Hannah went upstairs with him. Rishi was
to sleep on the third floor, where there was an
extra guest room and bath.

After they had gone, Nancy and her father dis-
cussed the mystery. Nancy remarked, "There are
several angles to consider, Rai's suspicious nature
and treatment of the boy and the search for
Rishi's father."

Mr. Drew agreed. "This is not going to be an

easy puzzle to solve. Nancy, we may have this boy here for some time. I notice he has no clothes except those he was wearing. I think we should borrow some for him. Is there a boy around here who's about his size?"

Nancy thought a moment, then said, "How about Bobby Allen down the street? You know his father well, don't you, Dad?"

Mr. Drew snapped his fingers. "A perfect suggestion." The lawyer went to the telephone and called Mr. Allen.

Without telling him about the mystery, Mr. Drew made his request.

"Indeed, my son would be glad to lend your visitor some clothes," Mr. Allen replied. "I'll let Bobby pick out a few things and we'll bring them over to you."

Within twenty minutes the two arrived with a suitcase full of clothes. The Drews explained to Mr. Allen and Bobby that the boy, whose name was Rishi, had already gone to bed.

"He'll try these on in the morning," the lawyer said.

While the men talked in the living room, Bobby went home. Nancy helped Hannah with the dishes and silver, then called Bess and George to tell them about the ivory charm she was wearing. The cousins were amazed by the news, but both declared Nancy certainly deserved it.

Bess added, "I hope Rai doesn't show up and take it away from you and hurt you in one of his fits of temper."

"I'll watch my step," Nancy assured her.

Finally all the lights in the Drew household were put out. Mr. Drew went softly to the third floor to check on Rishi. The boy was sound asleep and lying so quietly that it was evident that he was relaxed and happy.

The lawyer thought, "Probably the first peaceful evening Rishi has had in a long, long time."

Nancy could not get to sleep as easily as Rishi had. The specter of the towering Rai, decked in his long gown and turban, kept reappearing in her mind. She had laid his ivory charm on her bureau and wondered how long she might be able to keep it.

Her next thought was, "With Mr. Tilak away and Rai gone, what do I do next to solve the mystery?" She could not answer the question and eventually fell asleep.

The following morning, Hannah Gruen rushed into the girl's bedroom. There was a look of fright on her face as she said, "Rishi is gone!"

Nancy sprang out of bed. "What!" she exclaimed.

The kindly housekeeper said she had searched all over for the boy and even called to him but there had been no answer.

"Did you look outdoors?" Nancy asked her.

Mrs. Gruen admitted she had not. "But what would Rishi be doing outside for so long? He's been gone over an hour!"

Nancy quickly put on her slippers and warm robe. She followed the housekeeper down the stairs and went out the rear door. Rishi was not in sight. Then suddenly she startled Mrs. Gruen by laughing aloud.

"There's Rishi!" she said, pointing into the garage. "He's cleaning Dad's car!"

Hannah laughed, too, as she realized how much time she had wasted searching for the boy. It had not occurred to her to check the garage.

As she and Nancy approached, Rishi gave them a big grin. "Good morning. Rishi not sleep after five. Hunt for work to do. Nothing in house. Rishi come out here." With a twinkle in his eyes, he said, "Two cars very dirty. Rishi clean. Soon look like new."

Nancy thanked him for doing this good and necessary job, but Hannah scolded him gently. "You scared me. I've been looking all over the house for you. You should not have come out here without telling us."

"Nobody awake," the boy defended himself. "Rishi not write English. Could not leave note."

Hannah was sorry now for what she had said. She went to the boy and hugged him. "Forgive me, Rishi. I was so frightened I guess I became a little angry."

Rishi smiled. "Rishi forgive. Please, Mrs. Gruen, give Rishi breakfast. Very hungry."

"While we're waiting," said Nancy, "I'll show you a surprise."

She told him about the borrowed clothes. Rishi grinned and carried them upstairs to try on. In a few minutes he reappeared in pants, shirt, and a sweater that fitted perfectly.

"Now Rishi American boy," he announced, smiling broadly.

Soon everyone sat down at the table. There was orange juice and Hannah's special griddle cakes. Rishi enjoyed them.

In a little while Mr. Drew hurried away in his own car, saying he was going out of town for the day.

"Rishi go back to work, too. Wash Nancy's car now."

The boy stayed in the garage and once Nancy went to check on him. After he finished cleaning her car, he began to sweep the garage. Nancy thanked him.

She had scarcely returned to the house and started dusting the living room, when she glanced out a window and saw a green car turn into their circular driveway and stop in front of the house.

A woman alighted, and the man drove off. Nancy put the dustcloth away and when the front doorbell rang, she answered it.

A tall, willowy woman in her fifties with lots of blond hair stood there.

"I'm Mrs. Allison," she said rather brusquely. "I'd like to talk to Mr. Drew."

"Please step inside," Nancy requested. "My father is not at home. Is there anything I can do for you?"

"I'm afraid not," Mrs. Allison replied. "I must talk to him about a dream I had—— Oh!"

The woman was staring at the ivory charm Nancy was wearing. "Where——?"

The next moment she slumped down in a faint!

CHAPTER IV

A Baffling Caller

NANCY moved swiftly toward the stricken woman, but halted uncertainly as the front doorbell rang. She would have ignored it entirely had she not observed someone looking through the small glass pane. Had the person seen Mrs. Allison faint? At least the caller might offer aid.

Darting to the door, she flung it open. Without waiting for an invitation to enter, a tall, athletic-looking man strode into the hall. He was the one who had brought the woman.

"I am Steve Roach," he announced quickly, "Mrs. Allison's escort."

"You're just in time to help. She has fainted."

The stranger moved quickly into the living room and walked to the chair where the woman lay in a crumpled heap. To Nancy's amazement he lifted her up in his arms.

"I'm very sorry this happened," he said apologetically. "Mrs. Allison is subject to fainting spells."

"Will you please carry her up to a bedroom?" Nancy requested.

"Oh no, I'll take her to my car. She'll be all right in a minute or two."

"But she's as white as a ghost. You shouldn't move her in that condition."

Mrs. Allison stirred slightly in the arms of her escort.

"You see, she's coming around now," Mr. Roach said quickly. "Please let me handle this my own way. I understand Mrs. Allison far better than you do."

Nancy realized that it would be useless to protest. She held the door open for Mr. Roach, and with troubled eyes watched him carry the limp figure to a car parked in front of the house. He placed Mrs. Allison on the rear seat and drove away.

A few minutes later Nancy decided to go to the garage and see how Rishi was getting along with his work.

"Rishi almost finish," the boy said.

Nancy praised him for his excellent job, then asked, "Did you ever hear of a Mrs. Allison or a Mr. Roach?"

Rishi thought for a moment, then said, "Not hear of Mrs. Allison, but Rishi hear name Roach at animal show."

"You mean he's one of the performers?" Nancy questioned. Here was an interesting clue!

"Not perform," the boy replied. "Rishi hear Rai speak name Roach over phone."

"Do you know whom Rai was talking to?" Nancy put in.

Rishi shook his head. "Maybe Mr. Roach, maybe not."

Nancy's mind was leaping from one idea to another. Was Mrs. Allison looking for Rishi? Had she guessed Rishi might be at the Drew home? Had she fainted before broaching the subject? Had Roach also intended to ask questions but found his plans thwarted? And last of all, had Rai sent the couple there?

Suddenly a totally different possibility entered Nancy's mind. Mrs. Allison had fainted directly after seeing the ivory charm Nancy was wearing. Did its significance overcome her? Furthermore, Roach had probably noticed it. Would he tell Rai about it? The thought worried Nancy, but she decided not to mention it to anyone except her father.

She did, however, phone Mr. Strong to find out whether or not Rai had returned or if there was any news of him.

"No, unfortunately. How's Rishi?" the show owner asked.

"Very happy," Nancy told him.

Mr. Strong said his troupe would be moving

soon to a new location. "But I'll keep in touch."

That evening Nancy talked privately with Mr. Drew about what had happened. He frowned and said, "You have a right to be worried, not only for Rishi but for yourself. I don't trust those people if they're friends of Rai's. Please, Nancy, be very careful."

His daughter smiled and nodded. "Are you going to contact Mrs. Allison?"

"We don't know her address, but I'm certain we'll hear from her again."

The following noontime the lawyer phoned Nancy. "Hi," he said, "I have a bit of information that may interest you. It concerns your new acquaintance—Mrs. Anita Allison."

"She came to see you?" Nancy asked in surprise.

"No, but a real-estate dealer friend of mine, Mr. Howard, dropped into my office this morning. I gleaned a little information about the woman from him. She owns a house and grounds, which she had listed with him at a very high price. I learned its location. The property was left to her by her husband, but they never lived there."

"Where is it?"

"You remember the old Dawson farm east of River Heights?"

"Yes."

"Well, Mrs. Allison's property adjoins it. The

land includes several acres of forest, a creek, beautiful rolling hills, a ravine, and nearly everything essential to a good golf course. I think it might be sold for that purpose."

"I remember the place," Nancy replied. "Maybe Bess and George would drive out there with me. And Rishi, too, if you're willing."

"By all means take him along," her father urged. "The boy deserves an outing. But don't let him be seen in public, or Rai may spot him."

Shortly after lunch Nancy and Rishi picked up the cousins. Nancy drove directly east through the city.

"Where are you taking us?" Bess inquired with interest.

"To a new place." Nancy smiled enigmatically.

Rishi bubbled with enthusiasm and his gaiety was imparted to the others. He loved the outdoors and amazed the girls with his stories of country life in his native land.

He asked eager questions about the names of unfamiliar trees and birds he saw in the area. The girls were slightly embarrassed when they could not always answer him, and they resolved to devote themselves to nature lore with new interest.

"I'm ashamed that I don't know the names of half the birds I see," Nancy confessed. "I'll find out."

Presently the car passed the Dawson farm. Following the directions given by her father, Nancy turned into a narrow, winding side road that led between rows of tall elm trees and a tangled growth of shrubbery.

"I never dreamed there was a place like this so near River Heights!" Bess gasped in awe. "Who lives here?"

"It's Mrs. Allison's land, but she doesn't live here." Nancy told Bess and George how she had met the woman.

Nancy parked and they all got out. As they gazed across a picturesque creek, Nancy said, "Can you imagine yourself standing here and driving a golf ball over the water?"

"I can't," Bess replied, "because my ball would certainly plop into it."

"I'd want half of the trees cut down," George added.

"But what made you think of a golf course?" Bess asked.

"A realtor told Dad some people want to buy the place for that purpose," Nancy told her. "I suppose the old house would be torn down too and replaced by an attractive club building," she added, pointing to a large, apparently abandoned homestead, barely visible through the woods.

Bess and George both turned to stare. "Do you suppose it belongs to the Allison property?" George asked.

"It must. I'd love to explore the house," Nancy said, "but of course we have no right to. We're really trespassing as it is."

"At least it will do no harm to look at the outside of the building," George said. "Let's walk over."

"All right," Nancy agreed. "What became of Rishi?"

"He walked up this trail," George answered.

The trail led through the woods directly to the abandoned homestead. They emerged into the tiny clearing. Rishi was standing on the front porch, apparently trying to raise one of the windows.

"Rishi!" Nancy called sharply.

The boy wheeled. "Yes?"

"What are you doing?"

"No harm. Rishi only look at old house."

"I thought you were trying to get inside," Nancy said. "You have no right to do that, you know."

"Rishi think nobody care," the boy replied.

Nancy said no more. She and the other girls walked slowly around the house. The windows were placed so high above the ground it was impossible to see any of the interior.

"It's just an old, empty house, I guess," Bess remarked. "Let's go!"

The girls returned to the front of the building. Rishi had vanished.

"Where is he?" Nancy asked. "Do you suppose he dared to climb in that porch window?"

"Rishi had a mischievous look in his eye when he said he thought no one would care if he investigated," Bess reminded the others.

"He's probably inside," Nancy acknowledged.

The girls sat down under a tree to wait for him, but minutes elapsed and Rishi did not reappear. At length Nancy grew impatient.

"I'm going in there to get him! It's time we start for home."

She rose and walked briskly to the porch. Nancy knocked on the door but no one answered. Bess and George watched her raise the window and step through. Five minutes elapsed, then ten.

"What can be keeping Nancy?" George asked. "I think it's time I go after her. Want to come along?"

"I'll wait here. But let me know if there's anything interesting inside."

"I'll return soon," George promised.

Ten minutes later, Bess became convinced that something was wrong. Hurrying toward the house she called loudly, "George! Nancy!"

Her cries went unanswered. A sudden fear gripped Bess. She was certain that Rishi and her friends were being held prisoners inside the old house. If she were to enter, she too might be captured!

CHAPTER V

Hidden Rock Door

"I'll go for help!" Bess decided.

Almost overcome with fear and anxiety, she raced down the trail toward Nancy's convertible. Once she stumbled and fell headlong, tearing her slacks. She scrambled to her feet and ran on again.

Reaching the car, Bess was relieved to find that Nancy had left her keys in the usual hidding place. Bess started the motor.

"Where shall I go?" Bess wondered, starting to panic. She recalled having seen a farmhouse at the end of a nearby lane and decided to drive there for aid.

In her excitement Bess stepped too hard on the gas pedal and the car leaped ahead with a jerk, which flung her against the wheel. She slowed down. The road twisted and turned in a bewildering maze and seemed to lead into even wilder country. To the right, a short distance from the road, a high cliff of boulders and jagged rocks loomed up.

For an instant Bess's attention was fixed on the unusual formation. Then she stiffened, uttering a sharp, terrified scream. Her imagination evidently had not tricked her into believing that the center of one boulder had moved.

"It's a man-made door hewn in the solid rock," she thought, hardly daring to believe what she saw as the rock was slowly swung outward.

Intent on the strange sight, Bess suddenly lost control of the steering wheel. The car careened wildly in the road, then pitched heavily into a rain-gutted ditch.

The impact momentarily stunned the girl, but she recovered quickly and was relieved to discover that the car still stood on its four wheels, apparently undamaged.

A moment later Bess cried out, "Oh—the cliff! A boy's coming out of it!"

He emerged hastily and pushed the rock door back in place. He ran down the steep embankment toward the girl.

"Rishi!" Bess screamed, and then laughed in relief. "For an instant I thought you were a ghost!"

"Rishi no ghost. Very much real."

"You nearly made me kill myself."

"Rishi sorry," the boy murmured contritely. "You not hurt?"

"No, I'm all right, thank goodness. But I wonder if I'll ever be able to get Nancy's car out of this ditch?"

"Rishi push and it be all right, I think." He ran to the rear of the car but Bess stopped him in his tracks.

"First tell me if I'm dreaming," she said. "Did I actually see you come through a rock door in that cliff?"

Rishi nodded, politely waiting for another question from the girl before revealing any more information.

"But you were investigating that old place when I saw you last!" Bess exclaimed in bewilderment. "How did you get here? And what became of Nancy and George?"

"Rishi see no one in tunnel."

"You've been exploring a secret tunnel?" Bess demanded eagerly. "Does it lead from the abandoned house?"

Again the boy nodded. His brown eyes danced with excitement as he tried to explain.

"Rishi step through window in strange house. House have no insides."

"No insides? What do you mean?"

Rishi seemed unable to make himself understood. He groped for words.

"You mean it had no floor—no furniture?" Bess suggested.

"Yes, no floor, no insides! Steps lead down into

"The rock!" Bess cried out. *"A boy's coming out of it!"*

blackness. Then Rishi fall. Find himself at bottom of stone stairs. Long tunnel lead here. See light through crack. Push rock away."

Bess was bewildered by the boy's story, but thought his adventure offered a clue to the whereabouts of Nancy and George. Either in descending the stone stairway they had met with a mishap similar to Rishi's, or they had remained in the tunnel to investigate. Aware of Nancy's love for mystery, Bess was inclined to favor the latter theory.

"George and Nancy must be in the tunnel or the house," she declared. "Come, Rishi, show me how to enter through the rock."

Obediently he led the way up the steep bank to the boulder. He slipped his fingers into a crevice and pulled with all his strength. The rock did not move.

"Strange," he muttered. "Most strange. Rock move easy when Rishi push from other side." He tried again.

"Let me help," Bess offered.

Although the two pulled hard, it was impossible to budge the boulder even an inch. The secret door remained firmly in place.

"It's no use," Bess said in disappointment, giving up her efforts and resting. "We must return to the abandoned house."

Rishi hesitated, apparently afraid of risking further bruises.

"Nancy and George may be in serious trouble," Bess said urgently.

"Then Rishi go with you," the boy promised quickly. "But Rishi enter house in more safe way."

They returned to the car. Bess started the engine and shifted into low gear while Rishi pushed the convertible from the rear. The ditch was not deep, and with a low, rumbling protest, its wheels spinning in the dirt, the car lurched onto the road again. Rishi sprang inside, and Bess drove to the spot where Nancy had left the car before.

She and Rishi got out and ran along the twisting trail to the deserted house. In her anxiety to reach Nancy and George, Bess did not notice that Rishi was lagging farther and farther behind. Half walking and half running, she reached the place ahead of him and waited impatiently by the porch.

"Hurry, Rishi!" she urged, trying to catch her breath.

The boy eyed the building with obvious misgivings. "No need to go inside," he announced evenly.

"Nancy and George may be in serious trouble!"

"Not while Nancy wear wonderful elephant charm. If she meet bad trouble mystic power of charm save her."

Rishi spoke with a conviction that Bess could

not share. She was provoked by the boy's attitude, sincere though it might be.

"Oh, Rishi, you place too much trust in that ivory piece! I can't believe it has any unusual powers!"

"Ivory charm never fail," the boy insisted.

Bess was so exasperated, she felt like crying. She knew it would be impossible now to induce Rishi to reenter the strange house. She must investigate herself. But Bess, always more timid than her friends, was afraid to go in alone.

She stared at the building in a torment of indecision. Suddenly from far away she heard a cry.

"What was that?" she asked sharply.

The call was repeated. Bess thought she heard her own name.

With Rishi close behind, she ran toward the sound. Rounding an abrupt turn in the path, Bess nearly collided with Nancy. The girl's clothes were torn, her face was streaked with dirt, and her arm was bleeding from a scratch.

"Nancy!" Bess cried. "You're hurt!"

"You cut!" Rishi added.

"I'm all right." Nancy smiled. "But I've certainly had a strange experience."

"What became of George?" Bess asked.

"Isn't she with you?"

"No, When you failed to return she followed you into the abandoned house. I haven't seen her since."

"Then she must be somewhere in that wild labyrinth," Nancy answered, looking troubled. "I thought I'd never find the way out myself. My flashlight smashed when I fell. I kept walking and stumbling in the dark until I came to a queer door in a rock. It sounds impossible but it's true."

"I know it is," Bess said, "because I saw Rishi come out of that same boulder. He's been telling me a strange tale about the house having no insides."

The boy's eyes were glued on Nancy, waiting for her to answer.

"That's true, too," Nancy declared. "It's the weirdest, most fantastic place I've ever seen. Only I didn't see too much of it! It was almost pitch-black."

"George must be lost somewhere in the tunnel you and Rishi were in, Nancy."

"I'm afraid of that, Bess. We'll have to go inside and search for her."

"But we have no light," Bess reminded her. "If you and Rishi could find your way out, I'm sure George could."

Nancy agreed to wait a little longer. "Probably the wisest thing to do is to return to the boulder," she said after a moment's pause. "George could escape that way eventually and come back to the house."

Hastily the three returned to the exit of the tunnel and began their vigil. First, however,

Nancy convinced herself that Bess and Rishi were correct in saying that the mysterious door could not be opened from the outside.

Minutes elapsed and the lost girl did not appear. Bess and Nancy grew more worried, especially when they noticed that the sky was overcast with black, rolling clouds.

"Bad storm come," Rishi predicted.

"And it will soon be here," Nancy agreed. "I believe it's useless to wait any longer. Let's go back to the house and enter through the window."

Once more the three retraced their steps down the road and along the forest trail, coming at last within view of the abandoned house. In the gathering darkness it looked even more sinister and forbidding than it had before.

"I don't like the idea of going inside." Bess shivered.

"Neither do I," Nancy admitted, "but we must find George."

She moved boldly toward the front porch, with Bess and Rishi following reluctantly. Nancy paused to listen intently.

"It was only thunder," Bess said.

"No, I heard something——"

The sentence was never finished. From inside the house came a terrific crash accompanied by the sound of glass splintering against a hard, metallic surface. Then silence.

CHAPTER VI

A Web of Ropes

"Don't go inside!" Bess pleaded frantically. "Please don't. Something dreadful will happen to you!"

Nancy paid no attention. Boldly she flung up the window and stepped through the opening to find herself on a narrow ledge. She was startled to hear a low moan directly below her.

"George!" she called. "Is that you?"

"It's all that's left of me," a faint voice said with a groan.

Picking her way down the treacherous stone steps, Nancy descended quickly. When her eyes became accustomed to the gloom, she found George lying at the bottom, surrounded by broken glass. The girl's arms had been cut in several places.

"What happened?" Nancy gasped, mopping the blood with her handkerchief.

"Oh, I've had a horrible time!" George complained. "I got lost in a musty old passageway. When I found it was a dead end, I stumbled back the way I'd entered. Finally I reached the top of these steps and then slipped. I clutched at something hanging on the wall. It couldn't support my weight. I crashed down with it on top of me."

"Apparently you pulled a heavy mirror loose, George. You could have been killed."

"It sure was heavy," George answered ruefully, rubbing her head. With Nancy's supporting arm around her she slowly rose.

"Can you walk if I help you?"

"I think so."

Cautiously groping their way, the girls began to climb the steep stairway. Before they reached the entrance ledge, Bess thrust her head through the open window.

"Nancy! George!" she called fearfully.

"Here we are, directly below," Nancy shouted. "George has been hurt."

"Oh!" Bess exclaimed.

"I'm all right now," George insisted.

"Bess," said Nancy, "step inside onto a narrow ledge. See if you can find a light switch."

Nervously Bess entered and stood motionless on the tiny platform. Her fingers probed the wall until she felt a knob and turned it. Suddenly the room was flooded with light.

An amazing sight met their gaze. The house was indeed "without insides." The floor had been torn away. From the rafters of the ceiling hung several swings and trapezes, similar to those used in wild-animal acts, as well as many entangled ropes.

"What do you make of it, Nancy?" Bess asked in awe, as she descended the steps.

Nancy said she was puzzled. "This could have been a gym or even a place to train wild animals to do tricks."

George chuckled. "I can just see an elephant on a trapeze."

The other girls laughed, then Bess said, "Tigers can climb."

"Yes, tiger climb," came a voice from the open window.

Nancy glanced up. "Rishi! Step in and take a look."

While Rishi marveled at the strange sight, Nancy bound up George's cuts with a clean handkerchief and rubbed her bruises.

"Rain hard outside," Rishi said.

"Then we'll stay here until the storm's over," Nancy suggested.

Rishi began to test the ropes and swings. Bess uttered a little cry of alarm as the boy swung through space, hanging by his knees from the bar of a trapeze.

"He'll be killed!" she exclaimed.

Nancy warned him to be careful. "The safety net is broken," she cautioned. "And some of the ropes look very old and insecure."

"Rishi not take chance," he promised.

Outside the old house rain fell in torrents.

"While we're waiting, I believe I'll do a little investigating," Nancy said.

"We may as well go along," George added. "I feel okay now."

Leaving Rishi to amuse himself, the girls entered the secret tunnel. George found a light switch and clicked it on.

"One thing is sure," Bess remarked. "People come here. Otherwise the power would have been shut off. Why was this tunnel built, do you suppose?"

"That's what I'd like to find out," Nancy replied. "I have a feeling that so far we haven't delved very deeply into the mystery of this place."

As they moved down the tunnel, the girls came to a turn-off. Nancy paused a moment.

"I'm sure I must have taken the main branch before," she said. "Let's explore this one."

The passage she indicated was very narrow and so low that the girls were forced to stoop. It was dimly lighted. Suddenly Bess halted, gripping Nancy's arm. "What was that?" she said.

"I heard nothing."

"It sounded like a groan."

"You must have imagined it, Bess," George scoffed. "Not that I blame you. So much has happened I could start hearing things myself."

Unwillingly Bess moved forward again, slightly ahead of the others. She had taken less than a dozen steps when she stumbled over an inert figure stretched across the tunnel floor.

"Water! Water!" a man mumbled.

Bess wanted to turn and flee but could not do so with Nancy and George directly behind her, blocking the path. They, too, were startled, yet both realized that the man had been injured and needed attention.

Nancy knelt beside him, raising the victim to a sitting position. In the dim light she could distinguish only the faint outline of his face.

"Where are you hurt?" she asked gently.

"My head—I think it's broken. I was struck by a robber and dragged in here. But I'll get even! I'll fix him!"

Tired from speaking, the man dropped back against Nancy, a heavy weight in her arms. It was a full minute before she could rouse him again.

"Who are you?" she questioned. "Tell us your name and why you are in this house."

"I'm Jasper Batt. Old Batty, some folks call me. I look after the property."

"You mean you're the caretaker?"

"Yes, I've been here since the other guy was fired."

"Can you describe the person who struck you?"

"No," the man muttered. "He sneaked up behind me. I have a good idea who it was, though."

"Tell me his name," Nancy urged.

"No," Jasper Batt muttered. "I'll track him down myself. And I'll get my papers back, too!"

"Papers?" Nancy inquired alertly.

"Valuable documents entrusted to me by Rai."

"Rai?" the Drew girl exclaimed, believing that she had not heard correctly.

"I was to give the papers to Mrs. Allison when she came for them. If I don't, I'll lose my job."

"I'll help you recover them," Nancy said soothingly when she saw that the caretaker was becoming excited. "Only you must tell me more about the documents."

"Nothing to tell," Batt murmured, shaking his head from side to side. "I'll get the papers myself! I'll get even with that crook!"

He struggled to his feet, only to fall back once more into Nancy's arms, exhausted by the effort to rise.

"Leave me alone," he muttered angrily, kicking violently with his legs. "Leave me alone. Go away before I lose my job."

"The poor old fellow is out of his mind," Bess whispered. "What shall we do?"

"We must go for help," Nancy decided. "Come on!"

The three girls hurried back to the main tunnel, then made their way to the apparatus room where they had left Rishi.

Seeing no sign of him, Nancy called his name. The only sound she heard was the steady downpour of rain.

Suddenly George gripped Nancy's arm and pointed to the overhead web of ropes. Entangled among them, like a fly in a spider's web, hung a limp body!

"Nancy, that's Rishi!" George exclaimed.

The girls were stunned for a moment. They had no way of knowing how long Rishi had been hanging from the ropes. His face was so ashen-white that they feared he had strangled to death.

"We must go for a doctor," Bess gasped. The others knew this would take a long time.

Nancy's eye had been roving speculatively over the network of ropes. Several dangled from the rafters, one close to the entangled body of the boy.

If she could climb the adjoining rope she might be able to reach Rishi and cut him loose!

"See if you can find a knife or any sharp instrument!" she asked the girls. "Perhaps Mr. Batt has a pocketknife lying around here."

In vain the cousins searched for a knife. They were about to give up in despair when George spied a rusty old saw in a dark corner and snatched it.

In the meantime, Nancy had managed to climb the tricky ropes. Now she was endeavoring to reach a crossbeam directly opposite the rope from which Rishi dangled. George and Bess watched nervously as the girl swung herself toward the structure. She secured a grip with her feet, then went up hand over hand until she was able to climb from the rope to the beam.

Without waiting to be told what to do, Bess and George tied the old saw to the end of the rope Nancy had released, and she pulled it up.

"Nancy, be careful," Bess warned fearfully. "If you lose your balance it means instant death."

Nancy did not need to be told to use caution. She knew that one wrong move would prove fatal. Yet if she was to reach Rishi she must take the chance.

Clinging to the rope for support and with her feet on the beam, Nancy leaned forward. She reached out until she was able to grasp the boy's jacket. Nancy pulled the limp body toward her, lashing him fast to the crossbeam. Next she grasped the rusty saw and severed the rope that had entangled him.

"Is he still alive?" George called anxiously.

"I don't know."

Using another rope, which Bess and George

"Nancy, be careful," Bess warned fearfully.

swung up to her, Nancy tied it securely around Rishi's body. Next she severed those that held him to the beam, then slowly lowered the boy to the extended arms of Bess and George.

When Rishi was safely at the basement level, Nancy quickly slid down one of the ropes to join her friends.

"I'm sure he's dead," Bess whispered.

CHAPTER VII

The Tutor

NANCY kneeled down, felt Rishi's pulse, and pressed her ear against his chest. She could hear the faint beating of his heart.

"Rishi is still alive, but he needs resuscitation and stimulants. If only we had some medicine!"

In their anxiety for the life of the little boy, the girls had forgotten Jasper Batt. They were startled to see him emerge from the passageway, staggering as he walked toward them. His eyes had a wild, half-crazed expression, but the girls hardly noticed this. They were glad he was on his feet.

"Ask Mr. Batt if he has any medicine on the premises," Nancy urged her companions. She continued to work over Rishi, encouraged by the tiny bit of color that was returning to his face.

Bess and George questioned the elderly caretaker, and after explaining several times what they wanted, succeeded in making him comprehend them. He led the cousins to a medicine cabinet in a corner.

As George selected a stimulant, Bess said, "Mr. Batt, how are you feeling?"

"I kin walk, that's about all," he replied.

After Nancy had administered the stimulant, she was relieved to notice that Rishi's heartbeat became stronger. Soon he stirred and his eyelids fluttered open. He murmured something in his native tongue. Gradually he became aware of the little group around him and smiled at Nancy in recognition.

"Nancy save Rishi," he whispered weakly.

"Don't try to talk yet," she told him. "Just lie still and rest."

Rishi did not obey the order. His eyes fastened on the ivory charm Nancy wore around her neck, and he took hold of it.

"Rishi's life safe because of power in elephant charm!" he said.

"Please don't try to talk," Nancy advised again.

For some minutes Rishi remained quiet, gaining strength. Then, rousing, he indicated that he felt able to sit up.

The girls had paid little attention to Jasper Batt, knowing that he no longer needed their aid. They had actually forgotten his presence until he suddenly ran forward, waving a fist at Rishi.

"Now I remember! It comes back to me! He's the one who struck me!"

"Impossible!" George exclaimed. "You don't know what you're saying, Mr. Batt."

"Rishi is a friend of ours," Bess added.

"Rishi," the caretaker repeated. Obviously the name was unfamiliar to him. "No, he was the one!" he insisted wildly. "He told the other man to strike me."

"Only a moment ago you said that Rishi struck you," Nancy reminded him. "At first you declared you didn't see your attacker."

"This man was the person," the caretaker mumbled.

"Why, he's not a man at all—only a boy of twelve," Nancy cried.

"You are in league with him. You plotted with him to steal my papers! Give them back to me or I'll lose my job."

"The man is completely out of his mind," Bess murmured in an undertone. "Don't pay any attention to him."

It was impossible to ignore Jasper Batt, however, for he was quarrelsome and determined to make trouble. No amount of argument or explanation could convince him that Nancy and her friends knew nothing of the mysterious papers that had been stolen from him.

"You're all my enemies," Batt accused belligerently. "If you didn't come to trick and cheat me, why are you here?"

"We came to this house just to look around," Nancy said soothingly. "We'll leave immediately."

"Oh, no you won't!" the caretaker shouted. "Not until you hand over my papers. Give them to me."

"I tell you I know nothing of your papers. Try to be reasonable, Mr. Batt."

"If you won't give them to me, I'll take them!"

The caretaker seized Nancy roughly by the arm, and tried to thrust his hand into the pocket of her jacket. Bess and George, enraged, went to their friend's aid. The struggle lasted only a brief time, as Jasper Batt had not fully recovered his strength. He fell back against the wall, gasping.

"As soon as he regains his breath he'll be after you again, Nancy," Bess warned. "What shall we do?"

"We must get away from here before he becomes more violent."

Overhearing Nancy's remark, Jasper Batt moved swiftly to the foot of the stone steps. He believed that the girls intended to escape through an upper window.

"Oh, no you don't!" he sneered.

"We must slip out through the secret tunnel," Nancy whispered.

She helped Rishi to his feet, and with George

supporting him on the opposite side, the four moved stealthily into the passageway. Midway down the long tunnel, the girls paused to listen. They could not hear footsteps behind them.

"I hope we gave batty Mr. Batt the slip this time." George chuckled.

"Don't laugh until we're safely out of here." Bess shuddered. "What if the door in the rock won't open?"

This suggestion erased the smile from George's face, and she said no more until they reached the passageway exit. She groped about in the dim light and found a knob. The door opened easily, swinging slowly on huge iron hinges that had been drilled into the rock.

"Strange, the rock door can be moved only from inside," Nancy mused as they all emerged.

The storm had abated. Now, as they assisted Rishi to Nancy's automobile, the girls realized that a light rain was falling.

"How are you feeling?" Nancy asked the injured boy as she helped him into the car.

"Much better. But Rishi not try trick on ropes again."

"I should hope not! Only a miracle saved you from death. If we had found you even five minutes later——"

"No miracle," Rishi insisted firmly. "Ivory charm save life."

"If I were you I wouldn't trust this piece of

ivory too far," Nancy said. "As soon as we reach home you're going straight to bed, and maybe have a doctor."

By the time Nancy and Rishi arrived at the house, he had made such a noticeable improvement that it seemed unnecessary to call in a physician. Hannah helped the boy to bed and gave him some hot broth. He immediately fell into an untroubled sleep.

"I declare, Rishi has wound himself around my heart," the housekeeper confided to Nancy as they met in the kitchen. "I didn't realize how much he meant to me until this accident."

"We must plan for him to continue his schooling," Nancy said.

That night after dinner she brought up the subject of engaging a tutor to help Rishi with his English as long as he remained at the Drews'. As she had expected, Carson Drew instantly agreed.

"Select someone suitable and it will be perfectly satisfactory," he said. "I'll leave the matter entirely to you."

"By the way, Dad," Nancy said after a moment, "did Mrs. Allison ever call at your office?"

"No, she never did."

"I heard her name mentioned today in connection with Rai," Nancy told her father.

He glanced up with interest, and she told him the strange tale that Jasper Batt had related about the stolen papers.

"You're certain you heard the names correctly?"

"Yes, I'm sure I did," Nancy replied. "I suppose Batt must know Mrs. Allison well if she employs him to guard her property. It's possible, of course, that Jasper Batt was completely out of his head about stolen papers," Nancy admitted. "He certainly talked and acted wild enough."

"Even so, he must have heard Rai's name mentioned, or he wouldn't have repeated it."

Nancy nodded. "And another thing: when Batt first spoke of Mrs. Allison and the valuable papers he seemed fairly rational. It was later that he talked so strangely."

"Perhaps the old man's mind will clear and he can explain what he meant," the lawyer suggested.

"I think I'll give him a chance to settle down. Then I'll run out there tomorrow and talk with him again," Nancy said.

"If you do, be sure to take someone with you," her father cautioned. "Batt may be harmless enough in his normal state, but if he hasn't recovered from the blow on his head, he may give you some trouble."

"I'll be careful, Dad."

As it turned out, Nancy did not make the trip to the abandoned house on the following day. Another matter occupied her attention. Later the previous evening Ned Nickerson had phoned.

Nancy had briefed him on her exciting day and mentioned her plan to provide Rishi with a tutor.

"I know just the teacher for you," Ned said. "Professor Lowell Stackpole."

"It seems to me I've heard of him."

"Well, I should think so! He taught for years at Emerson College and is now retired. He's a traveler and art connoisseur. He has made at least ten trips to India and collects all sorts of native art. Professor Stackpole speaks several languages, including various Indian languages."

"Wouldn't he want more than we could afford to pay, Ned?"

"I don't know. But I think if Rishi interested him he wouldn't expect a very high fee. Would you like me to talk with him?"

"Yes, I would, Ned."

"I'll call Professor Stackpole tonight, and if the project appeals to him, I can introduce you to him tomorrow afternoon. How will that be?"

"Fine," Nancy agreed, immediately abandoning her plans to visit Jasper Batt.

Early the next morning Ned phoned to say he had arranged an appointment with the noted professor.

"He and I will come to your house at three o'clock," he promised. "Professor Stackpole wants to talk with Rishi before he decides whether he'll tutor him."

Nancy was excited over the approaching interview and hastened to tell Rishi the news. The Indian boy expressed appreciation for her interest, promising that he would study faithfully.

"As long as you keep ivory charm, Nancy, I do whatever you wish." He smiled.

"And if I should lose the charm?"

"Then bad luck follow you and me."

Promptly at three o'clock, Ned and the professor called at the Drew residence. Dr. Stackpole was a white-haired gentleman with a kind face. He carried himself well and his gait was that of a much younger man.

His bright-blue eyes glinted with interest as he shook Nancy's hand. She noticed that his gaze rested for a long moment on the ivory charm she wore around her neck. But he did not mention the carved elephant immediately.

At first the conversation was general, pertaining for the most part to Professor Stackpole's adventures in India.

"It is the most fascinating country in the world," he told Nancy. "You would love the temples and the great bazaars where native wares are bartered."

"I wish I might go there some day," Nancy said wistfully.

"You might find that many customs and practices would horrify you," Dr. Stackpole continued. "The old caste system has led to many social abuses. Then, too, in certain parts of the country the natives have no idea of sanitation. In the name of religion they bathe together in sacred rivers; some of the people are suffering from skin diseases."

"I'm glad I live in the United States," Ned interposed. "I understand that in India several different languages are spoken, among them Hindi, Marathi, Urdu, and Gujarati. Many communities have their own local dialect."

"That could make communication between regions difficult, couldn't it?" Nancy interjected.

The professor nodded, then said, "Some religions believe in reincarnation—that they are to be born many times. In some places children still marry at an early age. A girl unmarried at sixteen would be considered a disgrace to her family."

"I suppose certain natives place great faith in charms and omens," Nancy commented.

"Indeed they do. You might say that many of them are very superstitious. They believe in all sorts of miracles and sacrifices. One religious group, the Hindus, hold the cow to be sacred, another, the Parsis, worship fire. Many wear amulets and charms to ward off disease, preferring such protection to the services of a doctor. And there are natives who claim to have skill in black magic."

"I'm particularly interested in the beliefs held

in connection with elephants," Nancy interposed.

Again Professor Stackpole's eyes wandered to the charm worn around the girl's neck.

He explained, "The cult of the white elephant, practiced by the kings of Siam, probably had its origin in India and was based on the Hindu worship of *Airavat,* the sacred elephant of India. Even today one finds many charms made in the form of the elephant. Some are carved from pure ivory."

"Then ivory charms are somewhat common," Nancy observed.

"It depends entirely upon the workmanship. Some are very rare indeed. If I am not mistaken, that charm you are wearing came from India."

"It was given to me," Nancy said. "I've been very curious about its history."

"May I look at it?"

Nancy removed the charm from her neck and handed it to the professor for his inspection. He gazed at it so long without speaking that she began to feel uneasy.

"This is an unusual charm," he said at last in a tone that was almost reverent. "I have never seen one of better workmanship or quality. The ivory is pure, and I should judge very old. It has been carved by an expert. Nancy, you have a treasure!"

CHAPTER VIII

Woman in a Trance

"I HAD no idea the carving was so valuable," Nancy said.

"Unfortunately, I am not an ivory expert," Professor Stackpole said with a frown. "Yet it is obvious even to one with my slight experience that this charm at one time must have belonged to a person of great wealth—probably a maharaja. At any rate, your charm is valuable and should be safeguarded."

"I'll take good care of it," Nancy promised.

"The ancient ones are especially interesting," Dr. Stackpole remarked. "Some of them are said to have contained precious jewels; others held a poison to be used against enemies; and some, a unique life-giving balm."

"How could one tell the difference in the nature of the fluid?" Nancy asked curiously.

"The poison was dark in color, the life-giving

balm of light hue. But, of course, such things belong to the past. The modern charms have no cavities."

Nancy had been fascinated by Professor Stackpole's tales of India, but she did not forget the purpose of his visit. Rishi was summoned to meet the distinguished gentleman.

The boy's behavior was regal. Upon entering the room he joined his hands in front of him, palms together, fingers pointing upward, and bowed respectfully to the professor. Then, seating himself cross-legged upon a cushion, he conversed with the teacher in his own language. Professor Stackpole nodded approvingly from time to time.

After the boy had been dismissed, the tutor said warmly to Nancy, "It will be a pleasure to instruct him. He is unusually bright for his years, and I feel confident that he will make quick progress with our language. His English may be faulty but in his native Hindi he speaks with poetic beauty."

While Hannah served tea and cakes, Nancy finally brought up the subject of payment for Professor Stackpole's services. The gentleman named a sum so low that she felt inclined to protest.

"I tutor only because I enjoy the work," the professor explained. "If I had not thought Rishi could do it, I should have declined the task."

Before Dr. Stackpole left the house, arrangements were made for Rishi to begin his studies soon. The following day, after church, Nancy accompanied the boy to the professor's home, where he secured a list of the books that would be required.

"Rishi, you must study hard," she told him earnestly. "Kind Professor Stackpole will not teach you otherwise."

"Rishi burn much midnight oil." The boy smiled.

"If you learn other things as quickly as you do American phrases, I'm sure the professor will be highly pleased." Nancy laughed.

In the days immediately following, Rishi delighted everyone by devoting himself to his studies with great zeal. When he was not working about the garden, he would retire to his room, where he could often be heard reciting his lessons aloud.

The Drews were still worried about Rishi's so-called father, Rai. Nothing had been heard from him, and the police had no inkling as to his whereabouts. Since the animal trainer had vanished, tracing him was proving to be very difficult.

Nancy thought it might be wise in the meantime to visit the abandoned house again and see how Jasper Batt was. She also wanted to question the old caretaker about his knowledge of Mrs. Allison and Rai. Recalling her promise to Mr.

Drew not to go alone, she phoned Bess and George. Bess agreed to go but she would not enter the house. George was game for any adventure.

Early one afternoon the three girls drove to the Allison property. Nancy parked as close as possible to the empty house, then circled through the woods toward the building. They emerged from among the trees.

Nancy, who was in the lead, halted abruptly. Directly in front of the house, engaged in earnest conversation, stood a man and a woman.

"It's Anita Allison," Nancy whispered. "But I don't recognize the man. I wonder who he is?"

The three young detectives drew near the old house, making no secret of their presence, yet approaching quietly. Mrs. Allison and her companion were so engrossed in their conversation that they did not observe the girls.

"Your price, Mrs. Allison, is far too high," the man declared firmly. "We're willing to pay a fair sum for the place, but the amount you ask is unreasonable. As it stands, the property is useless to you, and in its present untended condition it is an eyesore to the community. If you sell to our firm you'll be doing River Heights a favor by making possible a fine new golf course, and at the same time you will assure yourself of a handsome profit."

"The stars are not in a favorable position for a

sale at his time, Mr. Bruce," Mrs. Allison said.

Nancy reflected that this was not the realtor who had been at her father's office.

"The stars?" the man repeated impatiently. "What do you mean?"

"I must have an omen. A favorable omen," the woman replied.

"That's ridiculous," Mr. Bruce snapped. "I never heard of such talk. This is a straight business deal."

"Your price is too low," Mrs. Allison insisted.

"You'll never receive a better offer. Ask anyone if it isn't a fair price. Consult Carson Drew—he knows the value of real estate."

"I'd rather consult the stars," Mrs. Allison said dreamily.

Mr. Bruce shook his head, baffled. Apparently he was at his wits' end in dealing with this woman.

"I must confess I'm at a loss to understand your attitude, Mrs. Allison. For the last time, will you accept my offer?"

"I am sorry. I cannot consider it at the moment."

"I warn you, Mrs. Allison, you may not have another opportunity. I will give you until tomorrow to change your mind. If you do, telephone me at my real estate office—you know the name —John Bruce."

The dealer turned and walked away indignantly. As Mrs. Allison stood staring indifferently after the man, the girls hurried forward. Nancy spoke to her, but realized instantly that the woman did not recall her face.

"I don't believe you remember me," Nancy remarked. "I am Nancy Drew—Carson Drew's daughter."

"Oh!" Mrs. Allison exclaimed in a strained, tense voice. "Now I remember. I was interested in——"

"A white ivory charm," Nancy finished eagerly, hoping the woman would acknowledge her interest in it.

She became aware that Mrs. Allison was no longer gazing at her. The misty brown eyes were fastened upon a faraway hillside, and a strange expression came over the woman's face. As if in a trance she began to murmur, "The elephant—the sacred elephant. Yes, yes, we were speaking of it—Rai and I—the sacred elephant!"

From a handsome white beaded bag, the woman removed a small gold-covered book. The girls could not take their eyes off it. They had never seen such a handsome volume. It was inlaid with semiprecious jewels spelling out the word "Sanskrit."

Nancy and her friends were further bewildered when Mrs. Allison began to chant sections from the tiny book in a musical voice. The passages she selected were elaborate, poetic translations.

Bess plucked at Nancy's sleeve, whispering nervously, "Let's get away from here. That woman gives me the creeps."

"She has some sort of psychic obsession," George added in an undertone.

Nancy was equally disturbed by Mrs. Allison's unexplained actions. The girl detective had never met anyone like her. Nancy had no intention, however, of leaving the scene. She believed that by listening intently to the passages she might pick up a valuable clue.

"Do read on," she urged Mrs. Allison as the woman paused.

Bess and George were completely baffled and a trifle annoyed by their friend's apparent absorption in the translations. They could make no sense of the passages, and after trying to listen for a time they became bored.

"I think Nancy has gone into a trance, too," Bess whispered to George. "Let's go off by ourselves until she recovers!"

The two girls slipped away quietly. Neither Nancy nor Mrs. Allison noticed their absence. The reading continued. Nancy was not bored. She listened, fascinated. The excerpts, which seemed to be taken from an ancient Hindu legend, related the tale of an Indian prince who had been spirited away from his parents. With her usual ability to make shrewd deductions, Nancy had gone directly to the heart of the situation.

"This story Mrs. Allison is reading must have something to do with the ivory charm," she reasoned. "And I believe it has a connection with Rai and Rishi."

Nancy had not forgotten Jasper Batt's hint that Mrs. Allison and Rai were acquainted. The woman might even know about Rishi's true parentage.

In her mutterings, Mrs. Allison spoke frequently of a little-known province of India. Nancy asked the name of its governor.

"Iama Togara," Mrs. Allison murmured dreamily. "He will rule with far more wisdom than his opponent. I have read it in the sands of time."

At this significant scrap of information Nancy turned to look at her friends. She was surprised to discover that they had gone.

"Tell me, Mrs. Allison," Nancy asked quickly, "is Rishi the son of a rajah?"

Before the woman could reply, an irritating interruption stopped her. Jasper Batt emerged from the house, walking directly toward the pair. Observing the man, Mrs. Allison seemed to recover from her trancelike state. She closed the gold-covered book and hastily replaced it in her purse.

"Is Rishi a rajah's son?" Nancy repeated her question hurriedly.

Mrs. Allison's eyes had lost their faraway expression. Now she looked at the girl with a cold, impersonal stare.

"I'm sure I don't know what you're talking about, Miss Drew."

By this time the caretaker had approached close enough to recognize Nancy.

"Oh, it's you!" he exclaimed in a quarrelsome tone. "I suppose you've come to make trouble. Well, scram before you get hurt!"

CHAPTER IX

Trespassers

UNAWARE of the reason for Nancy's interest in the Sanskrit poetry, George and Bess wandered some distance from the abandoned house.

"Suppose we take another look at that door in the rock," George proposed suddenly. "It may open from the outside if we can figure out the secret of how to operate it."

"Nancy may want to return home before we get back," Bess said doubtfully.

"Oh, she'll be listening to that woman for a long while yet. I never knew Nancy was so interested in psychic things."

The girls walked rapidly through the woods. Having selected a more direct route than the one that followed the road, they emerged at the high cliff. At close range the door in the rock was barely visible, but they knew its exact location and readily traced its indistinct outline.

"There doesn't seem to be a single thing to unlock," George commented after running her hand over the entire door. "It just isn't supposed to open from the outside, I guess."

Scarcely had she spoken, when the two girls were startled to hear a slight clicking sound. It seemed to come from within the rock. George and Bess fell back a step, staring in amazement. The door was slowly swinging outward.

Before they could recover from their surprise, a tall, muscular man emerged from the opening. He stood framed against the dark interior of the tunnel, holding the door to prevent it from closing behind him.

"What are you doing here?" he asked the girls gruffly.

"Why, nothing," George stammered.

"You must leave instantly."

As George and Bess turned to retrace their steps along the forest trail, the man commanded sharply, "Not that way!"

After shutting the door in the rock, he indicated that the girls were to follow him. He led them directly to the road.

"Follow this to the main highway," he instructed, scowling. "And never come here again without permission from the owner."

Bess and George scurried down the road, but at the first bend they paused to glance back. The man had not moved from his position. He was still watching them.

"Now how are we to find Nancy?" Bess asked when they were out of sight. "She'll be waiting at the house for us."

"If she doesn't return to the car we'll have to double back and take a chance on being caught."

"I don't want to meet that awful man a second time," Bess said.

By this time the girls had reached the parked automobile. They paused and were debating their next action when a figure emerged from among the trees.

"Nancy!" Bess exclaimed in relief. "We were frantic about you."

"And I've been worried about you," Nancy replied. "What happened to you?"

George quickly explained where they had gone and told Nancy about their unpleasant encounter. The cousins' description of the unfriendly man they had met fit that of Steve Roach, Mrs. Allison's escort.

"I wish you'd been with us," Bess said. "You would have found out something."

"I'd like to talk with Mr. Roach," Nancy said. "Apparently he has taken it upon himself to protect her property," Nancy concluded.

"Perhaps he's still at the cliff," George suggested.

Nancy glanced at her wristwatch. "It's late now and we really should be getting back to River Heights."

"Did you see Jasper Batt?" Bess inquired as they climbed into the car.

"Did you?" George chimed in.

Nancy laughed ruefully. "I certainly did! And in a most unexpected way!"

"Don't keep us in suspense," George said. "What happened?"

Briefly Nancy recounted the incident and noted that Mrs. Allison had been on the verge of revealing some important information.

"What do you suppose it was?" Bess questioned eagerly as Nancy turned the car into the main highway.

"I don't know. She wouldn't say another word after Mr. Batt appeared. It was provoking. I thought she was going to tell me something important about Rishi's parents."

The car was speeding along an open country road. Nancy slowed down for a curve. Then, to the surprise of her companions, she quickly stepped on the foot brake.

"Now what?" George demanded. "Don't tell me we have a flat tire."

Nancy shook her head and pointed to a large signboard in a field to the left of the road. "See that poster, girls! An animal show is coming here."

"Not to River Heights, though," Bess said in disappointment as she turned to read the sign. "It's at Hanover on the twentieth of this month."

"And that's tomorrow," Nancy added. "But what else does it say?"

"Oh!" Bess exclaimed. "It's the Bengleton Wild-Animal Show—the one Rai and Rishi were with!"

Nancy nodded. "Girls, let's plan to attend," she urged eagerly. "Maybe we can learn something about Rai from performers in the show. At least I hope so."

"I never turn down an invitation to anything exciting," George answered.

"I'd love to go," Bess added quickly. "Will you take Rishi, Nancy?"

"I'll see if he wants to go."

After dropping Bess and George at a supermarket, Nancy hurried home. This was Professor Stackpole's afternoon to tutor Rishi, and she wanted to talk to the distinguished man before he left the house.

As Nancy ran up the front steps, he was politely bidding Mrs. Gruen good afternoon. The door behind him closed.

"Are lessons over so soon?" Nancy inquired.

"Yes, it did not take me long to hear them. Rishi is a brilliant student."

"I'm delighted to hear that, Dr. Stackpole," Nancy replied.

"Rishi's mind never ceases to amaze me," the professor said. "His knowledge of the history of India is astounding, and he seems to be well versed in the traditions of various maharajas of India."

"I've often wondered if perhaps Rishi doesn't come from such a family himself," Nancy interposed quickly.

She half expected Professor Stackpole to laugh at the suggestion, but instead he regarded her soberly.

"That possibility has occurred to me also. Do you know anything about his parents or his life in India?"

Nancy described her first meeting with Rai and Rishi, adding a little of the evidence she had gleaned from Mrs. Allison. As she mentioned the Sanskrit poetry and the name of Iama Togara, Professor Stackpole's interest increased.

"Iama Togara is the governor of a small but wealthy province of India," he explained. "As I recall, the man ascended to power under rather peculiar circumstances, but the details have slipped my mind. If you wish, I'll look up the data for you."

"I'd appreciate it, Dr. Stackpole."

The tutor left. Before he was out of sight, the front door opened and his pupil emerged. The boy intently gazed at Nancy.

"Rishi have sudden premonition!"

"Did you learn that big word in your English lesson today?" Nancy teased.

Rishi appeared not to hear her. "I have strange premonition," he repeated. "Strange vision. Rishi see himself on way to India to become a great man. Big honor come through help of Nancy Drew!"

Nancy listened closely to hear more, but the Indian boy's reverie was interrupted by Hannah Gruen. Rishi immediately turned and went back into the house, without saying another word. Nancy whispered what the boy had been saying.

The housekeeper's only comment was, "Poor child! He dreams too much."

Nancy worked in the garden until her father came home. Making certain that Rishi was not within hearing, she told Mr. Drew about the Bengleton Wild-Animal Show at Hanover.

"If I can get away from the office, I'll run over with you," he promised.

"And perhaps you'd like to visit the abandoned Allison house?" Nancy asked, hoping he would. "It's on the way."

"All right," the lawyer agreed. "You've told me so many wild tales about the place, I admit I've grown curious."

Nancy was awake early the next morning. She helped Hannah prepare breakfast. Then, while waiting for her father to come downstairs, she unfolded the morning newspaper. Casually her eye scanned the headlines. Suddenly she uttered a startled exclamation that reached the far corners of the house.

"Dad! Hannah! Rishi!" she called. "Come and read this!"

CHAPTER X

Boxes of Treasure

"WHAT is it?" Mrs. Gruen asked, hurrying from the kitchen.

"Look at this paper!" Nancy cried, thrusting it into the housekeeper's hand. "The story about the fire."

By this time Carson Drew had come downstairs. "What's this about a fire?"

"Oh, Dad, Mrs. Allison's house burned down last night!"

"And a good thing in my opinion," Mrs. Gruen declared firmly, offering the newspaper to the lawyer. "That place was full of danger."

"Speaking of fires, I think I smell something burning now," Mr. Drew said, sniffing the air.

"Oh, my! The bacon!" Mrs. Gruen turned and fled to the kitchen.

Carson Drew quickly scanned the newspaper account. According to the story, the blaze had started during the night and was of unknown origin. A passing motorist had called the fire department, but before the firemen could reach the scene the building had been destroyed.

"It's too bad Jasper Batt didn't discover the fire in time to save the house," Nancy commented.

"From what you've told me of him, Nancy, he couldn't have been a very reliable watchman. Possibly the fire started from a match he carelessly dropped himself."

Nancy nodded soberly. "Or it may have been a case of arson. Perhaps someone wished to conceal forever the secrets of that strange house."

"Do you think Mrs. Allison would set fire to her own house?" Mr. Drew questioned his daughter.

"No, I hardly think she would do such a thing. I really have no theory about the fire. But I should like to drive out this morning and look at the ruins."

"Apparently you've forgotten that this is the day for the wild-animal show," Nancy's father reminded her.

"No, I haven't. We can go to Mrs. Allison's property first, then come back for Rishi. He has lessons now. I'll phone Bess and George and see if they'll be able to start early."

"The plan suits me," Mr. Drew agreed. "I've arranged to be away from the office all day."

Directly after breakfast Nancy talked with the cousins, saying she would pick them up at ten o'clock. Bess and George were waiting at the Fayne house when the Drews drove up. A short ride brought them within view of the Allison property.

Disregarding Steve Roach's recent warning not to trespass, the four walked rapidly through the woods to the clearing where the old house had stood. Now it was only a smoking ruin. Nancy's eyes roamed from the pile of debris to a lone figure working among the wreckage.

"Why, it's Mrs. Allison!" she exclaimed.

They hurried forward to find the woman trying vainly to move several half-burned timbers that blocked the stone stairway leading down into the secret tunnel. As Mrs. Allison turned to face the newcomers, her eyes filled with tears.

"You shouldn't be doing work like this!" Mr. Drew said. "If the timbers must be moved now, let me do it."

"I've been trying for an hour to get into the tunnel," Mrs. Allison half sobbed. "I am completely worn out."

"Why not wait until some of the debris has been cleared away?" Nancy suggested.

"Oh, you don't understand. I am afraid to wait even a day. Someone may steal my precious treasures."

"Treasures?" Nancy asked.

"They are hidden in the tunnel—many boxes of priceless articles. I must remove them before anyone comes. Oh, Miss Drew, if you and your father will only help me, I'll be so grateful."

"Of course we'll help," Mr. Drew said quickly. "If these timbers are cool enough to handle I think we can get into the tunnel."

"Wouldn't it be easier to enter the passageway through the door in the rock?" Nancy questioned, hoping the woman might divulge the secret of its mechanism.

Mrs. Allison glanced sharply at the girl. If it occurred to her to wonder how Nancy was so well informed about the tunnel, she refrained from saying so.

Instead, she murmured impatiently, "No, no. We cannot enter that way."

Fortunately, the portion of the basement in which the stone stairway stood had not entirely burned, so it was fairly clear of debris. In a short while Mr. Drew had dragged away the timbers blocking the passage.

"It isn't very safe to go in yet," he cautioned Mrs. Allison. "You might be overcome by fumes or heat."

"The air in the tunnel will be cool and clear," she insisted. "I must save my treasures! I have a big flashlight." She took it from her handbag.

"Then I'll go with you," the lawyer told her.

"But I feel that the undertaking may be dangerous. You girls remain here."

Bess and George looked relieved, for they had
been eyeing the great charred hole with misgivings. Nancy, on the other hand, could not
bear to remain behind.

"You'll need me to help you," she said to her
father. "And I have a flashlight, too."

"Oh, well, come along," he agreed.

Leaving Bess and George behind, the other
three swiftly descended into the tunnel. The
fumes were even more unpleasant than they had
anticipated. Both Mrs. Allison and Nancy were
choking and coughing before they reached the
cooler interior of the underground passage.

The woman went directly to a secret corridor
that branched off the main passageway. Using her
flashlight, she located a rectangular stone set high
in the wall. Her hand moved deftly over it to
touch a hidden spring.

Nancy and her father heard a faint click. Then
the woman tugged at the block and it slipped out
of its place in the wall. In the cavity were several
small boxes.

"Your treasures seem to be safe where they
are," Mr. Drew commented. "I doubt that anyone would ever suspect there was such a clever
hiding place."

"I can't leave the boxes here," Mrs. Allison declared. "They must be taken to a bank vault."

"That is the best thing to do," the lawyer agreed. "It shouldn't take us long to remove the boxes."

He pulled several boxes out and put them on the floor of the passageway, noticing their weight. He and Nancy wondered what the contents might be, but Mrs. Allison offered no information and they tactfully refrained from asking her.

Nancy bent down to pick up a small package, only to have Mrs. Allison say quickly, "No, I'll take that one."

As Nancy selected another box, her father lifted one of the heavy cartons. With Mrs. Allison bringing up the rear, the three started to carry their burdens along the tunnel.

Carson Drew, who was in the lead, suddenly halted. A loud, rumbling noise thundered through the tunnel, and a few loose stones overhead clattered down dangerously near their heads.

The lawyer pushed his daughter and Mrs. Allison back against the wall, saying sharply, "Don't move!"

The three huddled there for several minutes until the stones stopped falling. A thick cloud of dust filled the passageway.

"There's been a cave-in somewhere ahead," Mr. Drew said tensely. "Let's get out of here before we're buried alive."

"We can't leave my treasures behind!" Mrs. Allison cried in distress as she saw that Mr. Drew intended to abandon the boxes. "They represent a fortune!"

Considering the emergency, Nancy and her father thought that the woman was selfish to place her own interests above their lives. They knew, however, that it would take less time to carry out the boxes than to make Mrs. Allison understand the need to hurry. They picked up the boxes and rushed down the tunnel.

They were able to go only a short distance. Rounding a slight turn in the passageway they were dismayed to find it blocked by a pile of dirt, rock, and overhead beams that had given way.

"I was afraid of this!" Mr. Drew exclaimed. "We're trapped!"

"Oh, what shall we do? What shall we do?" Mrs. Allison wailed. "We'll never get out of here alive."

Sinking down on one of the boxes of treasure, she sobbed hysterically.

"The situation probably isn't as serious as it appears," Mr. Drew said with forced cheerfulness. "If we're unable to dig our way out, Bess and George may soon realize that something is wrong and send help."

Meanwhile, Nancy had been pulling and tugging at one of the half-buried timbers. "The cave-in doesn't extend far!" she cried. "We're

near the main tunnel entrance. I can see a faint
streak of light."

"You're right, Nancy," Carson Drew agreed
jubilantly. "We may get out of here by our own
efforts yet!"

The two started to work through the debris,
succeeding after some backbreaking labor in en-
larging the aperture slightly. But beyond that
point they could not budge the heavy beams.

"If I only had a few tools," the lawyer said
dejectedly as he sank down on the floor of the
tunnel to rest. "I fear we're trapped. We must
wait for a rescue."

Nancy measured the opening with her eye. "I
believe I could crawl through, Dad. If you'll help
a little, I'm sure I can make it. Let me try, anyway."

Before her father could protest, Nancy thrust
her head and shoulders into the yawning hole.
Midway through she became wedged fast. The
young sleuth squirmed and twisted, unable to
move either forward or backward. Then, by sheer
strength, Mr. Drew pushed her through to the
other side.

"I'll go for help," Nancy offered.

She ran to the main tunnel and was relieved to
find it clear. She raced up the stone steps, where
Bess and George were waiting.

"Come quickly and help!" Nancy pleaded.

"We're trapped!" Mr. Drew exclaimed.

"Mrs. Allison and my father are trapped in the tunnel."

"Trapped!" Bess gasped.

"Yes, in the branch-off. There was a bad cave-in."

Thoroughly alarmed, Bess and George followed Nancy down into the tunnel. For half an hour they worked hard to dislodge rocks and timbers. Without tools, it was difficult. Finally, however, the blocking beam was pushed aside. Mrs. Allison, pale and shaken, was lifted through, then Carson Drew followed.

"We must take the boxes," the woman murmured weakly. "I won't leave here without them!"

To quiet her Mr. Drew climbed back into the hole. One by one, he handed out the heavy cartons. The girls carried them from the tunnel.

George realized that a small box was slipping from under her arm. Just as she reached the end of the passageway, the box dropped to the ground and split open.

The contents, a collection of precious gems, flowed in a tiny river of sparkling color over the ground and down among the ruins!

CHAPTER XI

Bout With a Monkey

"OH, my treasures from India!" Mrs. Allison shrieked. "Save them!"

"I'm terribly sorry," George muttered. "Why didn't someone tell me I was carrying jewels?"

She turned to apologize further to the woman and was dismayed to see her sagging toward the littered floor in a faint. Mr. Drew caught her, easing Mrs. Allison down gently. Her eyelids fluttered open as Nancy bent above her, but the woman did not seem to recognize the girl.

"The treasure!" she whispered. "My precious treasure!"

Bess and George began to pick up the sparkling pieces of rare stones.

"Don't worry about your jewels," Nancy said kindly. "They're safe."

Mr. Drew added, "I'll take the boxes to a bank vault if you wish."

Mrs. Allison did not appear to comprehend. A dazed, faraway look came into her eyes and she muttered incoherently.

"What's the matter with her?" Bess whispered anxiously. "I never saw anyone act like this before."

"I think she's going into a trance," Nancy declared.

As minutes passed and Mrs. Allison made no effort to rouse herself from the state of semi-stupor, Carson Drew became impatient. He was inclined to believe that the woman made no effort to control her nerves and actually tried to create highly emotional scenes.

"Something must be done about these boxes," he observed. "I'll take them to a bank vault while you girls remain here. If Mrs. Allison isn't better by the time I return, we'll take her to a doctor."

The strange woman paid little attention as the jewels that had fallen out were gathered and replaced in the broken box. Mr. Drew asked Mrs. Allison the name of her bank. She did not appear to understand the question.

"Where shall we deposit the treasure?" he prodded. "Mrs. Allison, have you any preference as to a bank?"

"Please don't trouble me now," the woman murmured indifferently. "I am meditating."

After several attempts to discuss the matter failed, the lawyer said he would take the boxes to the River Heights National Bank.

Left alone with Mrs. Allison, Nancy and her friends tried to draw the woman out of her stupor. She did not respond until Nancy, hopeful of gaining information, deliberately mentioned Rishi's name. The word seemed to conjure up a strange train of mental pictures in Mrs. Allison's mind. She began to mutter again.

At first the girls could distinguish nothing, but as they bent over the relaxed figure, they caught enough to comprehend that Mrs. Allison was speaking of reincarnation.

"She's spooky," Bess commented. "Reincarnation means that after you die, you'll be reborn as another person or animal, doesn't it?"

"I'll probably be a goat!" George chuckled.

"Sh!" Nancy warned. She did not want to miss a word of what Mrs. Allison was saying. The woman lapsed into another silence, seemingly disturbed by the interruption.

"You were just talking about reincarnation," Nancy prompted quietly.

Mrs. Allison made no immediate response. Her eyes had focused on the elephant charm that hung from its velvet cord about Nancy's neck. With trembling fingers the woman reached out and touched it reverently.

"The ivory charm will bring you good luck," she murmured, "both in this world and the next. After death you will be reborn—you will enter a higher sphere and enjoy a life of splendor. You, Nancy Drew, will be reborn to become the beautiful wife of a rajah of India!"

Mrs. Allison lapsed into a moody silence. She closed her eyes, and the girls carried her upstairs and outdoors. She presently fell into a natural sleep from which she awakened fifteen minutes later.

"Dear me, have I been dozing?" she asked, looking about in bewilderment. "Where am I?"

"Don't you recall the cave-in?" Nancy questioned in amazement.

"Oh, yes, now that you speak of it, I do."

"Surely you must remember that we carried out several boxes of treasure," Nancy reminded her, "and that a small container of jewels was dropped on the ground."

Mrs. Allison's blank expression made it evident to the girls that the incident had left no impression on her mind.

"You don't remember anything you said to Nancy?" George asked.

Before Mrs. Allison could answer, Mr. Drew rejoined the group.

"You're looking much better than you were, Mrs. Allison," the lawyer remarked. "Are you all right now?"

"I feel quite my usual self, thank you. If you'll excuse me, I believe I'll go to my car."

"Just a minute," Carson Drew said. "Don't you want to hear where I took your boxes?"

"Boxes?"

"Yes, the treasure we carried from the tunnel. I deposited everything in a vault at the River Heights National Bank. Here's the receipt and your credentials."

Absentmindedly the woman reached for the papers.

"Thank you," she murmured. "Thank you for your trouble." Abruptly turning, she walked swiftly down the wooded trail toward her parked car.

"Well, is that all the appreciation we get for lugging out her heavy old boxes?" George demanded with annoyance, when the woman had disappeared from sight.

"I don't believe Mrs. Allison is entirely herself," Nancy said. "She's been talking wildly, Dad."

"I doubt that she understood what I was telling her," Carson Drew added with a troubled frown. "At any rate, I hope she doesn't lose those papers."

"Perhaps we can catch her before she leaves and explain matters again," Nancy suggested, following the woman.

They all ran to the roadside but Mrs. Allison

had driven away. Mr. Drew glanced at his wrist-watch and said it was not too late to attend the wild-animal show.

"I'd like to take Rishi," said Nancy. "Do you think he might be recognized, though, and there'd be trouble?"

"Let's chance it," her father suggested. "We might pick up a good clue."

When Rishi received the invitation, he was happy at first, then sobered. "Rishi afraid to meet Rai."

"I'm sure he isn't there," Nancy replied. "Mr. Strong promised to notify us if Rai returned."

"Then Rishi go," the Indian boy said. He changed his shirt and they all set off for the show.

The town of Hanover was crowded with cars, and the streets near the fairgrounds, where the huge tents had been erected, were jammed with people. While Mr. Drew parked the car, the others walked into the grounds. Soon they heard the first strains of carnival music and were approached by vendors of popcorn, balloons, and toy animals.

"The show will soon be starting," Nancy said, her anticipation mounting.

They could not hurry, however, as they moved along the lanes of caged wild animals. The three girls with Rishi elbowed their way through the throng, clinging to one another to avoid being separated.

As they approached the monkey cage, the crowd became even denser, drawn by the comic antics of the animals. It seemed hopeless to find Mr. Drew in such a mob.

"Oh, I see him!" Nancy cried presently. "Over there on the opposite side of the cage. Dad! Dad!" she called to him.

Before the girls could reach him, the crowd grew wildly excited, pushing and shoving in an attempt to move away from the vicinity.

"What's wrong?" George asked, clinging tightly to her friends.

She was told by a bystander that a careless guard had left the monkey-cage door unbolted, and now a dozen of the mischievous little animals were escaping. One athletic monkey perched himself atop the cage, two others clung to the outside wire network, while the rest began to terrify the crowd by leaping from one onlooker to another.

"Oh!" Nancy exclaimed.

One monkey had landed on her head and began pulling the girl's hair.

"Ouch! That hurts! Get off!" she cried out, trying to grab the frisky little animal.

All he did was squeak and pull harder. At first Bess and George giggled at the funny sight. But then George pulled the monkey's tail. This was not to the animal's liking, and he quickly abandoned his fun.

Rishi had become separated from the girls but now he returned in a flash. With a skill the bystanders could not believe, he coaxed the monkeys in a gentle, persuasive voice back into their trailer cage. The crowd cheered as he rejoined his friends.

The boy was embarrassed and said, "Rishi want to go now."

Nancy took him by the arm and hurried away, with Bess and George trailing them. They met Mr. Drew beyond the monkeys' cages. Nancy could not resist teasing her father.

"Dad, I'm surprised you'd deliberately unlock a cage door. Were you trying to get in with the monkeys?"

"At least no one has fed me any peanuts yet," Mr. Drew answered, grinning.

The show was just starting and Nancy's group hurried to locate their seats.

"I wish the elephant act would start," Nancy said to her father. "I can't wait to see who is in it."

"Your wish is about to be granted." Mr. Drew smiled. "Here they come now."

Nancy leaned forward. She caught a fleeting glimpse of the elephant trainer as he entered the big tent in full regalia.

"Is that Rai?" she whispered tensely. "It looks like him!"

Had Rai perhaps secretly returned without notifying Mr. Strong? Had he changed places with one of the handlers?

Rishi shrank down beside her and buried his head. "He mustn't see me!"

CHAPTER XII

A Startling Discovery

THE three jumbo elephants, guided by their trainer, had entered the ring directly in front of the section where Nancy and her friends were seated. The man turned to bow low to the audience.

"That isn't Rai, after all," Nancy murmured.

Hearing this, Rishi raised his head, and watched in fascination as the huge animals performed a series of perfectly executed stunts. In the final number, they climbed up on one another's backs to form a pyramid, as acrobats do.

As the applause died away, the beasts got down and lined up for a bow. The clapping was thunderous. Then, as the animals were about to trot from the ring, there was a sudden change from their placid attitude. The largest one stopped, raised his trunk, and began to trumpet loudly.

"Something is wrong!" Rishi cried. "That's old Arun!"

By now the elephant was making a beeline for a certain block of seats. The trainer was yelling at the animal. Guards were shouting, "Look out! He'll crush you!" and trying to keep the other beasts from stampeding.

Then someone yelled, "Arun smells Rai! He hates him!"

Rishi was already stepping across his friends' feet to get to the aisle. He reached it, leaped down the steps, and vaulted into the arena.

Nancy was alarmed. If Rai saw him, he might claim the boy and take him away before Rishi could find his rightful father!

She dashed after him but this was not necessary. Rai had left his seat hurriedly and scooted up the stairway to an exit. He disappeared.

By this time Rishi had reached the angry elephant and between trumpetings called softly to him. Old Arun stopped knocking over chairs in a front-row box and trying to step up among the panic-stricken, fleeing viewers.

"Arun! Arun!" Rishi pleaded, and added some soothing words in Hindi.

The elephant stopped his noisy outcries and backed up. Rishi gave a flying leap onto the elephant's back and sat down just behind the animal's head. Arun docilely joined his fellow elephants, and they all plodded peacefully out of the arena to the thunderous applause of the audience.

Nancy returned to her seat and ten minutes later Rishi came back. Everyone smiled at him but refrained from talking until the show was over. Then they praised him loudly, but the boy from India begged them to stop.

"Rishi glad to help. Lucky Rai not killed by Arun."

"And you're lucky," said George, "that Rai didn't have a chance to take you away."

Mr. Drew's group went to his car and drove off. It was late afternoon. The roads were still jammed with cars and the trip took longer than it would have under normal conditions. Consulting his watch, Mr. Drew announced that it was dinnertime.

"Let's stop at the next restaurant," he proposed.

The young people eagerly assented. In spite of the peanuts and popcorn they had eaten, they were hungry. Half a mile farther, Nancy noticed a brilliantly lighted restaurant just off the road.

"It looks all right," Mr. Drew commented, turning in at the driveway. "We may as well try it."

They entered the main dining room, which

was only half filled with guests. The group found a table for five near the window. After Nancy had made her selection from the menu, she glanced around at the other diners.

"There's Mrs. Allison!" she said quietly. The others turned to stare.

"It is!" George agreed. "And she's with Steve Roach."

"I'd like to talk to her," Nancy said impulsively.

"Perhaps you'd better wait," Mr. Drew cautioned. "Mrs. Allison and her friend seem to be having an argument."

The couple talked earnestly together, totally oblivious to the others in the room. Their voices rose higher and higher until Nancy and her friends caught enough to deduce that they were discussing the sale of Mrs. Allison's property.

"The argument seems to be nearly over now," Nancy observed presently. "If you'll excuse me, I'll go talk to them."

She approached the table at the opposite side of the room and spoke the woman's name. Recognizing the girl, Mrs. Allison made a pretense of welcoming her. Steve Roach scowled openly as he rose and offered Nancy a chair.

"I must apologize for interrupting your conversation," Nancy said, "but I have a rather important matter to discuss with you."

"Perhaps another time——" Mrs. Allison began.

"Oh, I didn't mean that I wanted to talk with you here, but I'm eager to get your present address so I can find you."

Mrs. Allison and her companion exchanged swift glances, which were not lost on Nancy.

"I move about from place to place," the woman answered vaguely.

"But surely you have a postal address. There must be some way for me to communicate with you."

"Just write a letter in care of General Delivery, River Heights," Mrs. Allison said.

Nancy was annoyed. The woman apparently did not wish to give out any information regarding her whereabouts. Nancy realized it would be useless to pursue the matter further, so she rose and said good-by. As Nancy returned to her own table, Mrs. Allison and Steve Roach immediately left the restaurant, without finishing their dinner.

"Where's Rishi?" Nancy asked, noticing that he had left the table and apparently taken his plate of food with him.

Mr. Drew shrugged. "He excused himself and said he would meet us at the car."

"Probably," George spoke up, "he didn't want Mrs. Allison or Roach to see him."

Her statement proved to be true. When the Drews and their friends returned to the car, they found Rishi seated on the floor of the rear seat.

"Excuse Rishi, please," he said. "Not wish to meet people Nancy speak to."

"I understand," Mr. Drew replied, and nothing more was said.

Bess carried the empty dishes back into the restaurant; then the group set off for River Heights. That evening Rishi studied for a short time before going to bed. Nancy briefed Hannah on the day's events.

"I have a little news, too," the housekeeper said. "A phone call came for Rishi. It was a man who didn't give his name. All I said was, 'There's no one here by that name,' and he hung up."

"Good for you, Hannah," said Nancy. "But *someone* must suspect he's here. We'll have to guard him very carefully." The housekeeper nodded.

The following morning, after Mr. Drew had left, Rishi went back to his studies. Hannah asked Nancy to do some marketing. The housekeeper went out to the garden to pick fresh flowers for the house. She found some weeds near the garage and decided to pull them.

"Oh, there's the phone," Hannah told herself.

She started for the back porch. By this time the bell had stopped ringing, so she turned back to her work. By the time she had finished, Nancy drove in and the two went into the kitchen to prepare lunch and chat.

"I'll call Rishi," Nancy offered, going to the foot of the front stairs.

The boy did not reply, so she mounted the steps and went to his room. It was empty. Not only was Rishi not there, but an open closet door revealed that his clothes were missing.

"Rishi has run away!" Nancy thought.

She looked for a note but none was in sight. Nancy opened the bureau and desk drawers. Still no explanation for the boy's disappearance. Suddenly she recalled the ringing telephone about which Hannah had told her. She raced downstairs.

"Hannah," Nancy cried out, "I'm afraid Rishi has been kidnapped!"

CHAPTER XIII

Coffeepot Cache

MRS. Gruen's mixing spoon clattered from her hand to the floor. "Rishi kidnapped!" she exclaimed. "This is dreadful! Who could have done such a thing?"

"I have a suspicion, but of course no evidence," Nancy replied.

"We must call the police at once!" the housekeeper insisted.

"I agree," said Nancy, and she hurried to the kitchen telephone. "I'll talk to Chief McGinnis personally."

After hearing the young detective's story, the chief offered to come to the house and get the details. He arrived shortly and was amazed by what he learned.

"Rishi was studying with Professor Stackpole, wasn't he?" the officer asked. "Do you think his

111

teacher thought the boy might be safer staying with him?"

Nancy shook her head. "The professor would never do such a thing. He would have asked us first."

Nevertheless, she phoned him. Dr. Stackpole was shocked to hear the news and declared he knew nothing about the kidnapping.

Chief McGinnis asked Nancy if she suspected anyone. "Yes. The man named Rai, who claims to be Rishi's father."

The officer said the police were still trying to locate the animal trainer. "But I'll put a couple of special detectives on the case."

After Chief McGinnis had left, Nancy and Hannah talked over the case. Nancy thought of two places to search.

"One is the home of Rishi's real father, the other is Mrs. Allison's property. Hannah, suppose you wait here for a phone call. I'll try to get Bess and George to ride to the other places with me."

In the meantime, Nancy called her father and learned he was out of town for the day. Next she phoned Bess and George, who gasped when they heard that Rishi had disappeared mysteriously, with his borrowed belongings.

Nancy picked the girls up a few minutes later and drove directly to the house occupied by the importer from India. No one answered the bell.

The same neighbor she had talked with before, Mrs. Wilson, told the girls that Mr. Tilak had not yet returned from India.

"Have you seen the boy who was with me around here?" Nancy asked her.

"No."

"If you do, please hold him until I can get here," Nancy requested.

"He's a runaway," Bess added. "In fact, he has been——" She stopped speaking abruptly as George gave her a withering glance. She was fearful Bess was about to say "kidnapped," an angle that was not to be generally revealed.

"If I see the child around, I'll invite him in, then notify you," Mrs. Wilson promised with a smile.

Nancy thanked her and the girls left. "I've decided to drive out to the Allison property and see if I can find Jasper Batt," Nancy announced as the girls entered the car. "I have a feeling he may know something about the kidnapping."

After a swift trip through the countryside, Nancy parked the car as close as possible to the ruins of the old house. The girls walked the remaining distance. Jasper Batt was busy raking up the debris around the burned mansion.

"I scarcely know how to approach him," Nancy whispered. "He may decide that I'm an enemy and attack us with that rake."

"We'll be on our guard," Bess declared. "If

he seems to be in an ugly mood we can always turn and run."

But this was not Nancy's idea of how to approach him. She put two fingers to her lips and the girls drew near quietly.

"How are you, Mr. Batt?" Nancy said pleasantly.

The man looked up and scowled. "Well, what do you want?" he demanded. "Can't you see I'm busy?"

"This will take only a minute, Mr. Batt," the girl detective began. "I want to talk to you about a boy named Rishi."

"I never heard of him. Go away and let me do my work."

"Very well, if that's the way you want it," Nancy said, humoring him. She turned as if to depart, then paused again. "By the way, Mr. Batt, did you ever recover those valuable papers you lost?"

"No, I didn't!" the caretaker snapped. "But I know what became of them all right!"

"I suppose you lost them accidentally?" Nancy prodded.

"Lost them! I should say I didn't. They were stolen by that no-good relative of mine. Name's Pete. He did it to get even with me because Mrs. Allison gave me his job of taking care of the place. Before I came here Pete looked after things."

"Pete?" Nancy inquired.

"Peter Putnam," Batt replied.

"Let me see, he lives near here, doesn't he?" Nancy probed.

"Too near to suit me. His place is about twenty miles beyond Doverville. You won't find Pete living in a regular house, though—not that guy. He's too stingy to build himself a decent place. He lives in an old barn that was standing on the property when he bought it."

Nancy asked several additional questions. Batt became suspicious that he was being pumped for information and refused to say any more. The girls returned to the parked car.

"I'd like to drive on to Peter Putnam's place," Nancy suggested. "Okay with you girls?"

"I'm curious to see his house," George answered.

Half an hour's drive brought the trio within the general vicinity of the Putnam farm. Upon inquiry at a gasoline station, they were told to follow a winding, rutty lane. The property was located nearly a mile from the main highway and consisted of a few acres of cleared land completely surrounded by dense woods.

"This must be the place," Nancy commented, stopping the car near a strange structure, which resembled neither a house nor a barn.

The queer, tumble-down building had originally been painted brick red, but now appeared to be washed-out pink. A porch had been built at the front, and large windows were cut into the walls at uneven angles. An old silo, long since useless, adjoined the east side of the structure, while the west side was supported by a massive stone chimney.

"Did you ever see such a crazy-looking house?" Bess giggled. "I wish I had a camera with me."

As the girls alighted from the car, a stout, short man in black corduroy trousers, a sleeveless leather jacket, and a misshapen, dirty felt hat walked from the building.

He removed a brier pipe from the corner of his mouth and demanded gruffly, "Yes? What is it? I warn you before you say a word that I won't buy anything."

"We have nothing to sell, Mr. Putnam." Nancy smiled, but added shrewdly, "We might be willing to make a purchase."

"Eggs, or a chicken?"

Nancy shook her head. "I'd like to discuss a business matter with you. May I come in?"

"All right," Peter Putnam consented grudgingly, "but the place ain't fixed up much."

"George and I will wait outside," Bess said hastily.

Nancy followed the farmer into the house and tried not to stare as she noticed how dirty it was. The huge rooms were nearly bare of furniture.

An old-fashioned cooking stove, a kitchen table, and a sagging cot were the main pieces. Peter Putnam drew up a crate, offering it to Nancy in lieu of a chair.

"What do you want to buy?" he asked eagerly.

"Perhaps I shouldn't have expressed it in just those words," Nancy countered. "I'm searching for some papers that disappeared from an old house owned by Mrs. Anita Allison. I'm willing to pay you for recovering the documents."

Putman eyed the girl cunningly; then he replied evasively, "Now what should I know about any such papers? Peter Putnam tends to his own business."

Nancy nodded. "You were the former caretaker at the Allison property. I thought you might be able to help me. As I said before, I'm willing to pay you to get them or tell me where they are."

"No doubt old Jasper Batt stole 'em!"

"I don't think so."

"How much are you willing to pay me?" Putnam asked cannily. "Mind, I'm not saying I could get 'em back for you."

"How about twenty-five dollars?" Nancy offered.

As she had anticipated, the sum sounded large to the miserly farmer. His face twisted into a grimace as he tried to decide whether or not to acknowledge that the papers were in his possession.

"Well, if I learn anything about the documents, I'll let you know," he said after a long pause.

Nancy had no intention of giving up so easily, but before she could think of a suitable response the two were startled to hear the angry barking of a dog in the yard. At the same instant, Bess uttered a terrified scream.

Nancy rushed to the window. An ugly white and brown mongrel had cornered Bess near the house and with menacing snarls threatened to attack her.

"Call off your dog," Nancy cried to Putnam, "before he bites my friend!"

Seizing a whip from a hook on the wall, the farmer ran out the door. Nancy attempted to follow, but in her hurry she tipped over an old coffeepot that stood on a sagging shelf near the window. It clattered to the floor and the lid fell back to reveal a white object hidden inside.

Bending down, Nancy picked up the coffeepot. She removed a long bulky envelope from it.

"What's this?" she wondered.

Had she made an important discovery? With trembling fingers she opened the envelope. Inside was another marked "Property of Anita Allison."

"These must be the stolen Allison papers!"

"*These must be the stolen papers!*" Nancy thought.

Nancy thought, quietly thrusting the envelope inside her jacket. Hastily she left the house.

In the meantime Putnam had driven away the hound, permitting Bess to escape to the car. Nancy and George joined her.

"We must get away from here at once," Nancy said. "If Putnam discovers I've taken the papers we want he'll try to stop us!"

"The papers stolen from Jasper Batt?" Bess questioned.

Nancy nodded, triumphantly tapping her jacket.

"I have the documents here. Let's hurry to a secluded spot where we can find out what they say."

CHAPTER XIV

Telltale Document

SEVERAL miles farther down the road, Nancy parked beneath an old oak tree. She opened the sheaf of documents and studied them eagerly.

"Don't keep them a secret!" Bess protested. "Did you get the right papers?"

"I'm sure I did. Some of these appear to be written in an Indian language, but the rest are in English."

"Is Rishi's name mentioned?" George asked, peering over Nancy's shoulder.

"I haven't seen it yet," she replied, then added quickly, "Yes, here it is!"

Nancy instantly grew serious. She spread out the English document so that her friends could read it, too.

"I can't make a thing of it," Bess complained. "The writing is too cramped."

"It says here that Rishi is the direct heir of a

maharaja of an Indian province called—oh, dear, I can't even start to pronounce the name of the place!"

"Don't try," George said. "Just give us the important details."

"As a baby, Rishi was abducted from his parents."

"Why was he taken away, and by whom?" George asked, trying to read the paper herself.

Nancy studied the writing for several minutes. "Girls, wait until you hear this! Rishi was deprived of his inheritance through the work of Anita Allison!"

"Mrs. Allison!" George exclaimed incredulously. "But if these papers belong to her, why didn't she destroy such incriminating evidence?"

"I think I can answer that," Nancy said. "According to this evidence, Rai was mixed up in the kidnapping and held these papers as a threat over Mrs. Allison. She in turn paid him blackmail money to keep him quiet but not enough to make the deal look suspicious. Finally, though, he sold them to her. For some reason he gave them to Batt to deliver. Before the caretaker was able to do so they were stolen by Peter Putnam. Naturally, if Mrs. Allison had received the documents she would have destroyed them immediately."

"But how did the woman become involved in such a disgraceful affair?" Bess mused.

"One guess is as good as another," Nancy said. "But I'd judge it was through her interest in mysticism. Perhaps she was under a spell and duped into it. At any rate, whatever her original motive may have been, she plotted to steal the estate of Rishi's parents and use part of the money to make Iama Togara governor of the province. In return for this, she received as a reward a priceless treasure belonging to Rishi's family. As I said before, this paper also reveals that Mrs. Allison, working with Rai, kidnapped Rishi. Everyone was led to believe that the infant Rishi had been devoured by a tiger."

"How dreadful!" Bess exclaimed.

"It sounds fantastic," George declared.

"I imagine," Nancy went on, "that Mrs. Allison kept the bulk of the loot but gave Rai the ivory charm. And just think! We helped her remove the stolen treasure from the secret tunnel!"

"Rai must be stupid to have accepted such an arrangement," George remarked. "I should think he would have protested."

"He is no match for Mrs. Allison, that's certain," Nancy replied.

"But why is the trinket so highly prized?" George asked.

"This document explains that the charm belonged to Rishi's grandmother. It was one of the most cherished pieces in the family and was believed to bring luck and health to the wearer."

"Nancy, harm may come to you as well as Rishi before we can find the boy," Bess said.

"Yes," George agreed. "Rai and Mrs. Allison will be terrified when they learn you found this document and took it."

Bess added, "Rishi's life may no longer be safe."

The girls rode off and were soon approaching the Allison property. Bess called attention to an oncoming car, which had turned into the side road leading to the burned house.

"Few people ever drive in there," Nancy said thoughtfully. "Do you suppose Mrs. Allison was in the car?"

"I couldn't tell from so far away," Bess replied.

"Now that I know she's involved in the plot against Rishi, I must locate her," Nancy continued. "It will take only a minute to stop and see who this person is."

Presently she drew up beside a sedan that had been parked near the burned house. The girls walked rapidly along the overgrown path until they came to the familiar clearing. Two men were talking with Jasper Batt.

"I've never seen either of them before," Nancy commented. "I wonder why they're here?"

Keeping out of sight, the girls moved forward quietly until they could catch snatches of the conversation. The men revealed that they were agents of the Reliance Insurance Company, sent by the local office to investigate the cause of the recent fire.

"Mrs. Allison is eager to have the claim settled as soon as possible," the girls heard Jasper Batt say.

"I can well understand that," one of the agents replied. "Unfortunately for Mrs. Allison the claim will not be settled, and she may consider herself fortunate if she avoids prosecution."

"What do you mean by that?" Batt demanded. "What has she done?"

The girls stepped closer so they would not miss a word.

"Our investigation discloses that this house did not catch fire accidentally," the other investigator went on. "It was deliberately burned."

"You can't prove it!"

"Yes, Mr. Batt, our evidence will stand up in any court."

"You can't show that Mrs. Allison or anyone connected with her set fire to the house. It was probably done by a prowler."

"We are not through with the case," the insurance man replied grimly. "By the way, Mr. Batt, we have come here today to ask you a few questions. Where were you at the time the fire started?"

"Look here!" the watchman cried furiously.

"You can't hang this thing on me. I don't know anything about it. I told you my idea of the fire—the house was burned by a prowler."

At that moment Jasper Batt glanced up and saw Nancy and her friends. His ruddy face twisted into an ugly expression.

"Question those girls if you want to know who started the fire!" he exclaimed. "They are always snooping around this place. I suspect they were the ones who struck me over the head and stole my papers!"

At mention of the word papers, Nancy glanced uneasily at her companions. She knew that if the lost documents were found on her, explanations would be hard to make! Not showing her fright, however, she walked boldly forward to speak with the insurance agents.

"Mr. Batt is not telling the truth," she said. "My friends and I have no knowledge of how the fire started. The day before the house was destroyed, we found Mr. Batt unconscious inside a tunnel. He told us then that he'd been struck over the head by an assailant who took his papers."

"That's true," Bess added. "Later, Mr. Batt began to accuse everyone of stealing the documents."

"Incidentally," Nancy went on, "he mentioned an old enemy—a former caretaker at this house named Peter Putnam. The two, I'm told, were bitter rivals, and there was some bad feeling between them because Putnam was discharged by Mrs. Allison."

"It's a trumped up story!" Batt cried.

The two insurance men had been impressed by Nancy's straightforward manner.

"What is your name, miss?" one of the agents inquired.

"Nancy Drew. You may have heard of my father—Carson Drew."

"We certainly have! If you're his daughter there's no need for explanations."

"Then we'll return home." Nancy smiled.

The agent said, "We may need you later to offer evidence in the case. If so, we'll call you at your home."

"Thank you," Nancy replied. Then the girls hurried off.

"You certainly walked out of that neatly," Bess remarked, when the girls were on their way to River Heights. "I was afraid the missing papers might be discovered in your possession!"

"Jasper Batt is too stupid to think of such a possibility," George remarked.

After Nancy had taken George and Bess to their homes, she drove to her father's office. When she reported the day's adventures, he was deeply impressed by the information contained in the documents she spread on his desk. The lawyer suggested that she show them to Professor Stackpole.

"I'll phone now for an appointment," Nancy replied.

After a brief pause she was connected with his residence, only to be informed that the man had left the city for a couple of days.

"How disappointing!" Nancy commented as she carefully placed the documents in her father's safe. "Now I must wait until he returns."

"In the meantime we'll make every effort to locate Rishi," Mr. Drew said. "Unless we find him again, your papers will not be of much value."

Both Nancy and her father were hopeful about tracing Rishi with little difficulty. Their first move was to communicate with the Bengleton Wild-Animal Show. They were disappointed to learn that the local police had obtained no clues either to Rishi or to Rai.

Given the possibility that the animal trainer had sought work with another outfit, they canvassed the state. No one had heard of Rai.

"The search will prove more difficult than I had anticipated," Mr. Drew admitted. "No doubt Rai suspects we may try to track him down and is hiding."

When Professor Stackpole returned from his trip, Nancy lost no time in calling at his home.

After relating the details of Rishi's disappearance, she placed the important documents in the tutor's hands. He pored over them for nearly an hour.

"This is indeed amazing," he declared. "Amazing! Yet I cannot say that I am greatly surprised. From the first time I met Rishi he impressed me as a boy of great refinement and unusual ability."

"Then you believe the documents are genuine?" Nancy asked.

"Yes, I do not question them. In securing these papers, Nancy, you have accomplished a remarkable bit of detective work."

"I'm sure Mrs. Allison is responsible for Iama Togara's becoming the governor," she said. "However, I want to get an admission direct from Mrs. Allison."

"But will that be possible?"

"I have a plan, Dr. Stackpole. Will you help me?"

"I'll do anything in my power to help. I've become very fond of Rishi."

"Then this is my scheme. By some ruse, please invite Mrs. Allison here to your home. You might say you wish to consult her about Indian mysticism. She'll feel flattered at the request and accept, I'm sure."

"And if she does accept?"

"Try to get her to admit that she helped to place Togara in power."

"But I haven't your ability as a detective."

"In this case you'll succeed where I could fail. Mrs. Allison would never talk frankly with me. She will be flattered by your interest."

The scholarly man nodded thoughtfully. "The plan might be worth trying," he admitted.

Nancy was delighted and said, "With your permission I'll eavesdrop on your conversation. If Mrs. Allison refuses to talk, then I'll appear and confront her with the documents."

"I'll attempt to make the appointment immediately," the professor promised.

"Thank you very much," Nancy said, rising.

Two days elapsed before she received word from the tutor.

"At last I have contacted Mrs. Allison," the professor reported. "I located her through a friend, Mrs. Winter, who happened to mention knowing her. Mrs. Allison has agreed to call at my home on Tuesday at three o'clock."

"That's great!" Nancy exclaimed. "I'll arrive ahead of her."

Nancy could hardly wait for Tuesday to arrive. In the meantime, however, she became busy getting ready for a weekend party at Ned Nickerson's fraternity house in Emerson. Bess and George had been invited but could not go because they had promised to perform in a play for children.

Once Nancy wavered in her decision to attend.

"I could be working on that mystery," she thought.

But when Ned phoned and she hinted at such an idea, he promptly said, "Nancy, you *must* come, not only for my sake, but perhaps to let someone here help you with your mystery. I want you to meet a boy from India."

There was no longer any doubt left in her mind about going.

CHAPTER XV

Stolen!

By Friday Nancy's enthusiasm for the weekend at Emerson rose to a high pitch. She eagerly looked forward to meeting the student from India.

When Nancy arrived in her car at the fraternity house, twenty girls were already there. After meeting Mrs. Howard, a pleasant, motherly woman who was the housekeeper, she was introduced to her roommate. Helen Heyman was a shy, timid girl. She confessed that she had never attended such a party.

"I'm so scared I'll do something wrong."

"Don't worry. You'll love it," Nancy assured her.

The following day the girls were rushed from one activity to another. Nancy met so many new students that she could not remember the names of half of them.

Ned's fraternity brothers had not forgotten

her, and that evening at the formal party held in the chapter house they annoyed Ned by constantly cutting in on his dances.

"I think you've danced with everyone here except Anil," Ned complained good-naturedly to Nancy. "That's the punishment a fellow gets for bringing a popular girl."

"Who is Anil?" Nancy inquired.

With a nod of his head, Ned indicated a handsome youth in evening dress who was standing at the opposite side of the room.

"He's the one I want you to meet. I'll bring him over."

Ned soon regretted that he had ever made such a suggestion. After Anil had been introduced he proceeded to monopolize Nancy's attention. He captured her interest by immediately mentioning the ivory charm she wore.

"It is a remarkable keepsake," he declared. "I have seen none to compare with it—even in the collections of the old maharajas of my country."

As the conversation continued, Ned tried in vain to divert Nancy's attention to himself. She listened with absorbed interest as Anil told her about Indian customs that were so different from those in the United States. The attractive student in turn gazed at Nancy as if he thought she was the most beautiful girl he had ever seen. It became increasingly clear to Ned that Anil was suffering from a severe attack of love at first sight.

At length Ned could endure it no longer. "Nancy and I have this dance," he told the young man.

"Very sorry," Anil apologized, smiling. He bowed to Nancy and moved away.

"I thought you were going to talk about the mystery," Ned complained.

"It wasn't necessary," Nancy replied. "I picked up some information from him that will help me."

Ned was not the only person present who had noticed the Indian student's infatuation. Some of the girls had overheard part of Anil's conversation and teasingly asked Nancy if her ivory charm was responsible for such attention.

Soon Nancy was dubbed "the girl with the ivory charm," and many asked to inspect the lucky piece. She was embarrassed by the notoriety, and was glad when the dance ended. Nancy said good night and went to her room, tumbled into bed, and did not awaken until the morning sunlight streamed in at the windows.

Her roommate had already left, and Nancy quickly started to dress. Suddenly she became aware that the ivory charm was no longer around her neck. Had she removed it the previous evening, before retiring? She could not remember doing so.

She searched the dresser, the bed, her suitcase, and finally in desperation told the other girls of her loss. Everyone joined in the hunt, but the charm could not be found anywhere in the house.

"Do you suppose that foreign student, Anil, could have stolen it?" a girl suggested.

"Oh, no!" Nancy exclaimed instantly.

"But he was interested in the charm. Everyone noticed it. And you said yourself that he spoke of its value."

Mrs. Howard, the housekeeper, did not feel so confident that Anil was innocent. Without telling Nancy, she telephoned him. After asking several pointed questions about the charm, she requested that he call at the chapter house as soon as possible.

A little after nine o'clock, Ned drove up hurriedly to the door and asked for Nancy.

"I've just heard from Anil about your losing the ivory charm," he said quickly. "But I'm sure Anil had nothing to do with the theft. The poor guy is almost beside himself with worry."

"I didn't accuse Anil," Nancy said in amazement. "I know he didn't take the charm."

"Mrs. Howard phoned him," Ned explained. "I suppose she meant well, but Anil thought he had been accused of the theft. He intends to run away before he's arrested."

"We must stop him, Ned."

"You're the only one who can explain to him, Nancy. That's why I came for you."

"I'll be ready in an instant."

She ran back into the house for her handbag. Bidding Mrs. Howard and the girls a quick good-by, she rejoined Ned. He drove swiftly to Anil's apartment house, but was informed that the young man had departed.

"Which way did he go?" Ned asked.

"Down Fulton Street toward the railroad station."

Nancy and Ned resumed their pursuit, and a few blocks farther on were gratified to glimpse Anil trudging along with his heavy suitcase. Ned halted the car at the curb.

"I did not steal the charm!" Anil cried out, before either Ned or Nancy could say a word. "Let me go in peace, I beg you!"

"We don't want you to go, Anil," Nancy said. "It's all a mistake."

"You have found the charm?"

"No, but Mrs. Howard didn't mean to accuse you of taking it. We all know you're innocent. There is no need for you to run away."

Anil blinked back tears of relief. When he tried to express his thanks words failed him.

"You are very good," he murmured at last. "Very kind. I will do all I am able to help you recover the charm. Now that it is gone your good luck is supposed to end."

Nancy smiled. "I've always been considered a lucky person, even before receiving Rai's charm."

"Rai?" Anil asked.

"Yes. You know him?"

"Only casually. I have met him a few times. Last evening he telephoned me."

Ned and Nancy exchanged significant glances. Here, they thought, was an unexpected clue.

"Was this after the dance?" Nancy asked.

"Yes, he called my apartment."

"And by any chance did you mention my name?"

Anil was surprised at the question. "Yes, I did," he admitted. "I told him of your wonderful personality."

"And my ivory charm?" Nancy prompted.

"I did mention it, I believe."

"I think that explains everything," Nancy said quietly to Ned. "My bedroom at the fraternity house is on the first floor and I slept soundly."

"I did not mean to reveal anything of importance," Anil said in alarm. "What have I done?"

"It isn't your fault," Nancy assured him. "However, I'm afraid Rai took my charm. Tell me, where is he now?"

"I have no idea. He telephoned from a hotel

and mentioned that he was leaving the city in an hour."

"Don't look so glum, Anil," Ned told him. "No one blames you. Jump in the car and we'll take you home."

En route, Anil repeated over and over that he was upset at the outcome of the casual telephone call.

"Don't take the matter too seriously," Nancy urged as they parted. "I have faith I'll find the ivory charm, and after all it did belong to Rai."

During the ride back to the fraternity house, neither she nor Ned talked much. Both felt discouraged and blue.

"I guess the weekend was a failure, after all," Ned said as Nancy alighted at the Omega Chi Epsilon door.

"No, it wasn't. I had a wonderful time."

"But you lost your ivory charm."

"It's a clue to Rai's whereabouts. My first move when I get home will be to trace him."

The next day elapsed, however, without any word of either Rai or the missing Rishi. Mr. Drew had devoted many hours to the case, but had been confronted with defeat at every turn.

"Rai must have a secret hideout," he told Nancy. "Otherwise, we'd surely locate him."

"At least we're still in touch with Mrs. Allison," Nancy answered, "and I have the incriminating documents that will convict her. And this is the day of Dr. Stackpole's appointment with her."

"You must be very careful about what you do or say," the lawyer cautioned. "You are getting into deep water."

"Not so deep that I can't swim out." Nancy smiled confidently.

A few hours later, en route to Professor Stackpole's residence, she did not feel so courageous. She knew that Rishi's future as well as her own safety might depend upon the outcome of the meeting with Anita Allison.

Could the young detective prove to be a match for the clever woman?

CHAPTER XVI

Nancy's Masquerade

NANCY was escorted into Dr. Stackpole's private study, where she found him nervously pacing the floor.

"Ah! I am glad that you have arrived early," he said in relief. "To tell you the truth, I am beginning to wonder if we have made a wise move in inviting Mrs. Allison here. Something may go wrong. Then serious consequences could result if we have made a mistake."

"But she's guilty of kidnapping, Dr. Stackpole. The documents in our possession prove that. And she is a thief as well."

"Yes, that is so. But if Mrs. Allison suspects that her true character has been exposed, she may resort to violence. I am afraid for your sake, Nancy."

"I'll be on my guard," Nancy promised. "Just show me where I am to hide."

Unwillingly the elderly man led her to an alcove just off the study, which served as a tiny solarium. It was filled with palms and potted plants, offering an excellent hiding place where Nancy could hear and see everything without being detected. She chose a nook behind a large pottery vase.

The girl had just secreted herself when the doorbell rang. Dr. Stackpole hurried to answer it.

He was utterly unprepared for the sight that greeted his eyes. Mrs. Allison was wearing a long flowing white costume and turban, and carried a jewel-bound book in her hand. She entered as if walking in a trance.

"This way," the professor stammered, moving toward the study.

He offered Mrs. Allison a chair, which she ignored. She stared at her host with a glazed expression.

"You are interested in mysticism?" she murmured, before the dazed professor could speak. "We are, I believe, of one spirit in this matter. I shall read that we may find communion together."

With one arm outstretched in a dramatic gesture, Anita Allison began to read from the jeweled volume. Nancy knew by the blank expression on Professor Stackpole's face that the man was too stunned by the exhibition to comprehend a word. But by the time Mrs. Allison had finished the passage he had recovered his usual poise.

"A beautiful quotation, Mrs. Allison," he said. "But our time is short and we must talk of India."

"Ah, yes." The woman sighed. "India—the land of adventure and mystery. What tales I could tell of its glamorous rulers!"

"Perhaps you could tell me of Iama Togara," Dr. Stackpole suggested cautiously. "I fear the stories that filter to us in the West are but half-truths."

"The real story of how Iama Togara became a great power has never been told," Mrs. Allison boasted. "You would not believe me were I to say that I aided in making him both maharaja and governor."

"Indeed I would," Professor Stackpole answered.

"The untimely death of a maharaja's heir, a boy named Rishi, left the community affairs of the province in a hopeless muddle," Mrs. Allison explained sadly, dabbing at her eyes with a handkerchief. "I was deeply grieved over his demise."

"I can imagine you were!" Nancy thought scornfully.

"Rishi's mother died of a broken heart, and his father emigrated to a foreign country when a near revolution among his workers started. One thing led to another and the entire province was plunged into turmoil," Mrs. Allison continued. "I knew that someone strong would have to be found quickly if war were to be avoided. I decided to act—you understand that I was motivated entirely by my desire to aid the poor people."

"Oh, certainly," Professor Stackpole murmured, trying to hide his contempt for the woman.

"Through various political and psychic connections I was able to place Iama Togara in power."

"And your reward?" Dr. Stackpole inquired. For the first time Mrs. Allison regarded him with a slight trace of suspicion.

"Nothing," she answered shortly. "I did it because of my warm feeling for India."

Professor Stackpole encouraged her to reveal more. As it became apparent, however, that she was regarding his interest with distrust, he switched to another subject. He spoke of a certain type of carved Indian vase that had intrigued him.

"I have tried to buy such a vase at various art stores," he remarked, "but I can't locate one that pleases me."

Mrs. Allison nodded understandingly. "I know exactly the sort of work you mean, and it is difficult to obtain. I have a friend, though, from India, who might be able to find the vase for you."

"You are very kind. I don't suppose your friend could be a man named Rai?"

Again Mrs. Allison regarded the professor suspiciously. "Certainly not," she replied stiffly. "I have never heard of him."

By this time it was evident to Nancy that Mrs. Allison was entirely too wary to say anything that might involve her in the scheme to deprive Rishi of his rightful inheritance. More drastic methods would have to be employed to compel the woman to confess.

The girl detective slipped quietly through a window and walked around to the front door. She rapped. A maid promptly answered and led her into the library.

Immediately Nancy took a deep breath as she entered and apologized for intruding on the pair.

"We were just having a pleasant little chat about India," Dr. Stackpole said. "Mrs. Allison is considered an authority on the subject of mysticism."

"How interesting!" Nancy exclaimed. "I have always been deeply intrigued by that subject myself. In fact, some of my friends believe that I have psychic powers."

"Indeed," Mrs. Allison remarked.

"Yes," Nancy continued glibly, "I have always felt that I had the ability to look into the past. Under correct conditions, I have faith that I could demonstrate this strange power."

"Psychic powers are far more rare than you think," Mrs. Allison said unpleasantly.

"Nevertheless, I am certain I have them. If you wish, I will prove it."

The woman hesitated. Then, before she could speak, Professor Stackpole said quickly, "By all means, Miss Drew. Such a demonstration should prove interesting."

"Lower the blinds," Nancy requested.

When the room was shrouded in semidarkness she said to Mrs. Allison, "I must have your turban."

"This is nonsense," the woman complained as she unwillingly gave up the round, banded silk hat.

After placing herself in front of a dark velvet drapery, Nancy closed her eyes. She began to rock slowly back and forth, chanting in low, musical tones. At first her words were unintelligible. Then she began quoting passages from the documents she had taken from Peter Putnam.

Mrs. Allison leaned forward, gripping the arms of her chair. Her eyes dilated with fear. She tried to speak, but made only a choking noise in her throat.

Nancy knew it was time for the climax. She took a step toward the woman, and her hand swept outward in a gesture of accusation.

"*You* are the guilty person!" she proclaimed. "You deprived Rishi of his right to become a maharaja and brought him to this country. Confess! Confess!"

For an instant Mrs. Allison seemed too stunned to move. Then she dropped down to her knees before Nancy, sobbing wildly.

"Yes, yes! I did it. I employed Rai to kidnap the boy so that Iama Togara might be put in power! I did it for India!"

"You kidnapped Rishi because your reward was a precious treasure," Nancy corrected sternly.

Before Mrs. Allison could reply, there was an unfortunate interruption. A telephone rang in the adjoining room.

Mrs. Allison straightened. The look of fear left her face and she became composed.

"I must answer," Professor Stackpole murmured as the ringing continued.

Nancy realized that the spell was broken and expediently emerged from her "trance." She had secured the confession she wanted. The professor would serve as a reliable witness against Mrs. Allison at the proper time.

"Well, did my psychic demonstration convince you?" Nancy smiled.

"It did. I—I don't suppose you remember much of what you said?"

Nancy was not compelled to reply, for Professor Stackpole appeared in the doorway just then.

"The call is for you, Nancy. Your father wishes to speak to you."

Nancy hurried to the telephone. "What is it, Dad?" she asked.

"I really shouldn't have bothered you," the lawyer apologized. "I merely phoned to learn if you're safe. Since you left I've been worried. By the way, Ned was here looking for you."

"I'm all right, Dad. Everything is going great. Only I can't take time to tell you about it now. I'll call you back in a few minutes."

Nancy cradled the phone and returned to the library. She paused in the doorway to stare in horror. Professor Stackpole lay stretched out on the floor, unconscious. His head was bleeding from a deep wound. Mrs. Allison had disappeared!

CHAPTER XVII

A Maharaja's Son

"Mrs. Allison did this!" Nancy thought as she ran to the professor's side. "That awful woman was afraid he would reveal to the police what he'd heard!"

Just then the front door bell rang. Instead of going to answer it Nancy called loudly for help.

"Coming!" a masculine voice shouted from the kitchen.

The next moment Ned Nickerson ran into the room, but stopped short as he saw the professor lying on the floor.

"What happened?" he asked.

"Dr. Stackpole is badly hurt," Nancy cried frantically. "I guess he was struck with this heavy bookend." She pointed to one that lay nearby. "We must give him first aid!"

She and Ned worked silently over the aged professor, and were relieved that his heartbeat seemed regular, although weak.

"He'll be all right in a few minutes, I think," Ned said after a time. "But we need ice or a cold compress."

"I'll see if I can find the maid," Nancy offered.

She went to the kitchen. Neither the cook nor the maid were there, but the refrigerator contained an ample supply of ice cubes. The caller at the front entrance had been forgotten, and he did not ring again.

Nancy was searching for a plastic bag in which to put the ice when she heard a slight noise at the kitchen door.

"Come in!" she called.

The door opened and there was a gasp of surprise. Nancy turned.

"Rishi!" she cried.

The boy laughed in relief and joy. "I ring front bell. Nobody answer."

"Oh, I'm so glad to see you!" Nancy exclaimed, then asked, "Why are you here? Why didn't you return to my house?"

"Rishi afraid Rai look there for him. Rai in this city now. He trail me like dog."

"Then you were wise to come here," Nancy acknowledged. "Rishi, a few minutes ago Dr. Stackpole was injured."

While she was explaining what had occurred, Ned appeared. He was wondering what had detained Nancy and was greatly startled to see the young boy. With the professor in urgent need of attention, however, there was no time to exchange introductions or to hear Rishi's full story of who had captured him, how he had escaped from Rai, or where Rai might be found.

"Dr. Stackpole is conscious now," Ned told Nancy. "But I need the ice."

They returned with it, followed by Rishi. When they had ministered to the elderly tutor, they were able to lift him to a couch.

After a time the man's strength returned and he gazed about the room, trying to locate objects and persons. Rishi stood gazing sorrowfully at his stricken tutor.

"Is it really you—Rishi?" the injured professor asked in a barely audible voice.

"Yes, yes," the boy said eagerly. "It is me, Rishi. I mean—it is I," he stammered, trying to use the correct grammar the man had taught him recently.

"I shall always be proud that I served as your tutor," Professor Stackpole said in a half whisper. "The lost son of a maharaja!" he murmured weakly.

Rishi stared at Nancy in bewilderment as if expecting her to offer an explanation for the man's strange words.

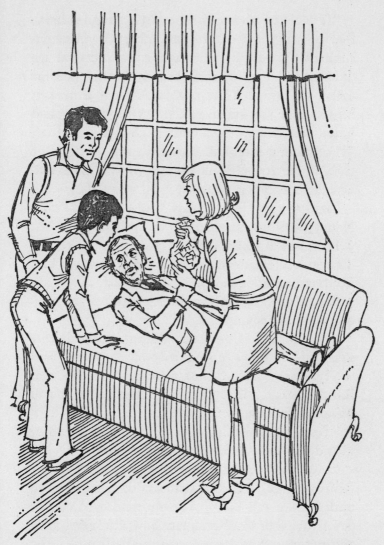

"The lost maharaja," *the professor murmured.*

"It is true," she told him. "We have evidence that proves you were kidnapped from your own country by persons who had great political influence and made Iama Togara both governor and a maharaja. Your mother died of a broken heart when she received word that a tiger had killed you. Your father left the country."

For a long moment Rishi did not speak. But tears of joy trickled down his brown cheeks as he eyed Nancy with a worshipful gaze.

"Rishi very happy boy now. Thank you, Nancy, for find out truth."

Professor Stackpole slowly rose from the couch. "If you will excuse me, I shall retire to my room. My head aches severely."

"Shouldn't we call a physician?" Nancy inquired anxiously.

"No, no, I will be quite all right after I have slept." The man moved toward the door and then paused. "Rishi must remain with me until Rai and Mrs. Allison are apprehended. He will be safer with me."

"Yes," Nancy admitted. "I doubt that they would think of searching for him here."

"I will ask the maid to prepare a room for Rishi at once," Dr. Stackpole said. He bowed to both Nancy and Ned. "You must forgive me for deserting you in this manner. I am very tired and not myself."

After the tutor had gone to his room, Nancy and Ned told Rishi the details of Mrs. Allison's plot against him. The boy in turn described Rai's cruelty toward him during the boy's captivity.

"He keep me in small room. When he go away even for one hour, he bind me to chair so I no run away again. Rishi not have enough to eat. Every night he beat me for go to Nancy. Say take me far away. Be in new animal show. Today I work and untie ropes and run away."

"Good for you!" Ned told him with a grin.

Nancy said sympathetically, "You've had a bitter experience, Rishi. But I'm sure you'll be safe as long as you remain with Dr. Stackpole."

"Rishi stay very close in house." The boy smiled. "Never go outside again until Rai is capture."

Nancy rose to leave. It occurred to her to ask Rishi if during his period of captivity he had observed Rai wearing the missing ivory charm.

Rishi shook his head. "Never see it."

"I'd give a great deal to get hold of that lucky piece," Nancy remarked. "Somehow I can't help but feel that the story is true, and the charm guards a strange secret."

"Rai often say same thing," Rishi said gravely. "Once he say charm have power of life or death."

"That was a queer remark," Nancy mused. "I wonder——"

She left the thought unexpressed, and after bidding Rishi good-by, departed with Ned and spent the rest of the evening with him.

The next morning Nancy slept a little later than usual. She had just finished dressing when Hannah called up the stairway that Nancy was wanted on the telephone.

"I think it's Dr. Stackpole," the housekeeper said. "He seems greatly excited."

Nancy had an extension on a table alongside her bed and picked it up.

"Hello. This is Nancy."

"I have distressing news for you," the professor told her in a strained, tense voice. "During the night Rishi disappeared from my home!"

"Kidnapped?" Nancy asked.

"I don't know. I blame myself, Nancy. I should have watched the boy more carefully."

"This is dreadful!" Nancy cried. "I'll talk to my father about it."

She put down the phone and flew to the dining room, where Mr. Drew was eating breakfast. In terse sentences she revealed what had occurred.

"The case has gone far enough," the lawyer responded grimly. "It calls for drastic action." He jumped from his chair.

"Shall we notify the police?" Nancy suggested.

"We'll do more than that. I'll call the FBI."

Within minutes Mr. Drew was in touch with a

friend in the Federal Bureau of Investigation. He returned to Nancy who in the meantime was thinking along totally different lines.

"Dad," she said, "this is about the time when the importer from India is supposed to return to River Heights. Do you think Rishi has gone there to see Mr. Tilak?"

CHAPTER XVIII

Amazing Reward

M<small>R</small>. Drew looked at his daughter, startled. "Nancy, you may have guessed the answer. Call the house at once."

Nancy did so. A woman answered the phone and said she was expecting her employer within the hour.

"Is a boy there waiting for him?" Nancy asked.

"No. No boy is here."

"Thank you," Nancy said and hung up. She hurried back to her father and told him what she had learned. "Dad, I want to go over there anyway and meet that man. Will you come along?"

"Glad to. I want to hear his story and see if it jibes with that of Mrs. Allison."

Twenty minutes later the two set off. When they rang the bell of Mr. Tilak's home, a woman answered and said he had returned.

"I'm Mr. Drew and this is my daughter Nancy," the lawyer said. "We live here in River Heights and would like to speak with your employer."

"Step inside," the woman said. "I'll tell him. Please sit down."

As she disappeared up the stairway, the Drews had an opportunity to glance around. The furnishings were beautiful and all of them apparently from India.

"It looks like a museum," Nancy whispered. "What gorgeous ivory figurines and rugs!"

In a few moments Mr. Tilak came down the stairs. His resemblance to Rishi was so startling there was no doubt in the Drews' minds that he was the boy's real father.

After greeting his visitors, he asked, "You wish to speak with me?"

Mr. Drew nodded and said, "Nancy will tell you."

"I hardly know how to begin," she admitted but decided to plunge directly into the story. "When your Rishi was a baby, you were told he had been killed by a tiger. This was not true. He was kidnapped!"

As she paused, Mr. Tilak leaned forward in his chair and gripped the sides. "Yes. Go on."

"Did you ever hear of a man named Rai?"

"No."

"Or a Mrs. Allison?"

"No."

Mr. Drew spoke up. "They are the culprits and also are guilty of starting a revolution in the community over which you held so much influence. You were driven from your country so that Iama Togara could take your place. The wealth stolen from your estate was then used to elect him as governor of your province. Nancy found secret papers to prove this."

The former maharaja jumped from his chair. "Is my son alive?" he asked.

"We hope so," Nancy replied, then revealed what had happened to Rishi and how the Drews had become involved in the case.

Mr. Tilak was speechless with surprise and dismay. Nancy's father told him the local police and the FBI were hunting for Rishi, Rai, and Mrs. Allison.

"We should have some word soon," he assured the boy's father, as the Drews rose to leave. "Mr. Tilak, we'll let you know the instant we hear anything about Rishi."

Before Nancy said good-by, she looked at Rishi's handsome but sad-looking father. "I would like to tell you about a remark Rishi made. He said if he ever found you, he was to say 'Manohar' to you."

The man gave an exclamation in Hindi, then apologized and said in English, "If I needed any proof you do know my son, this is it. Manohar was the name of the manager of my estate when I was a maharaja. He was killed during the revolution."

Mr. Tilak shook hands with the Drews and thanked them profusely. Then they left.

The lawyer told Nancy he would go directly to his office, phone the bank, and instruct them not to let Mrs. Allison take the contents of the safe deposit box. Instead they were to notify the police and hold her until they came.

Nancy drove into town with him, said good-by, and set off for home on foot. All day long she restlessly waited for news but none came. Toward evening she decided to walk downtown and meet her father.

"I'll go by way of the park," she thought, turning into it.

Her mind had reverted to Mrs. Allison. If she is around River Heights, what an ideal secluded spot it is. It could remind her of her burned house. And what an auspicious place to go into a trance!

After a moment the young detective smiled. "It would probably be a little used section of this park. I know the very place!"

Nancy headed for a densely wooded area. An old wooden footbridge crossed a deep, rushing stream. She paused, startled.

Not twenty feet away, the figure of a woman loomed up. She wore a white turban, and the wind whipped her flowing robes about her wildly. As Nancy watched, the strange person approached the bridge railing. She stood there transfixed, gazing down intently into the angry water.

"That's Mrs. Allison!" Nancy's body tensed at the thought. "Is she going to jump in?"

The girl detective stole forward, being careful not to make a sound. The woman, unaware that anyone was approaching, stood motionless, still gazing moodily into the stream.

"What shall I do?" Nancy wondered.

She was tempted to run to Mrs. Allison, but reflected that Rai might be in the vicinity. She would be no physical match for the two, and they would certainly capture her!

"I must phone the police," Nancy reasoned.

Stealing away quietly, she ran to the nearest street telephone booth and asked for Chief McGinnis. Nancy tersely revealed her information to him and was assured that men would be dispatched at once to the bridge.

"Maybe you'd better approach the place quietly," she warned. "Otherwise, Mrs. Allison may be alarmed and try to escape."

After completing the call, Nancy quickly returned to the bridge. Mrs. Allison had not moved. Greatly relieved, Nancy secreted herself in a clump of bushes nearby.

"I'll wait here for the police," she decided.

The minutes dragged by slowly. Nancy grew

worried and impatient. Then she heard the muffled sound of an engine. A car stopped some distance from the bridge.

Apparently Mrs. Allison had caught the faint hum. She glanced about alertly.

Officers were moving stealthily along the footpath now. The woman turned as if to flee in the opposite direction. Nancy emerged from her hiding place to block the way.

Mrs. Allison knew she was trapped.

"No, no!" she cried out.

The suspect wheeled, and before anyone guessed her intention, climbed the high rail of the bridge.

"Stop! Stop!" Nancy screamed, sure Mrs. Allison intended to make a dangerous jump.

The woman poised on the rail for an instant. Then she plunged into the water.

CHAPTER XIX

Dangerous Dive

NANCY darted to the railing. She could see Mrs. Allison struggling in the current, which was carrying her swiftly downstream.

"She can't swim!" Nancy thought frantically. "Or else she hit her head."

Nancy mounted the rail and carefully made a shallow dive. Shaking the water from her eyes, she looked around. Mrs. Allison was still struggling, but the thrashing of her arms was rapidly growing weaker.

A dozen powerful strokes brought Nancy to the woman. Approaching from the rear, she tried to grip her in a safe cross-chest carry. Mrs. Allison fought feebly to elude her rescuer.

"Let me drown! Let me drown!" the woman pleaded.

Nancy's only reaction was to tighten her hold under the woman's armpit.

The swift current had carried the two far downstream. For a minute Nancy allowed herself to drift with it as she caught her breath. Then, with her free right arm, she struck out again and reached shallow water just as two policemen rowed up in a boat. They relieved Nancy of the woman and took them both to shore. Mrs. Allison was escorted to the police car.

"Miss Drew, we'll need you along to offer evidence," one of the men said. "You can get some dry clothes from the matron at headquarters."

Half an hour later, Nancy met Mrs. Allison in the chief's office. The woman's attitude seemed to have changed entirely. As the girl detective began to question her, this became more apparent. Mrs. Allison had lost some of her former arrogance and answered certain questions readily.

The burned house had been headquarters for a circus troupe long before her husband had bought the property. Mrs. Allison's visit to see Mr. Drew had been coincidental. Someone had told her he was unusually good at divining strange cases, and she had had a frightening dream.

"I don't have to confess any more until I get a lawyer," she said. "But I'm sorry about Rishi," she mumbled. "I don't know what made me do what I did."

"Tell us where Rishi and Rai are now," Nancy said.

"Rishi has been hidden at the burned house," Mrs. Allison admitted. "Rai and Jasper Batt are guarding him."

Nancy did not wait to learn more. She was afraid that Rishi might have been harmed. Accompanied by a few policemen she drove directly to the place. The officers searched the premises thoroughly.

"No one is here," they reported to Nancy, who had waited in the car.

"You searched the tunnel?"

"Yes, it is empty. Mrs. Allison evidently lied."

Sick with disappointment, Nancy was forced to return home while the policemen went back to headquarters to report their failure. Carson Drew met his daughter at the door and heard her vivid account of the evening's adventure.

"Great work, Nancy, capturing that woman," he said. "But I shudder when I think that she might have drowned you."

"My life-saving course took care of me, Dad," Nancy replied with a half smile. "It was disappointing not to find Rishi. I was so certain Mrs. Allison was telling the truth."

"Perhaps Rai moved the boy to another hiding place without informing Mrs. Allison," Carson Drew suggested.

"That's possible," Nancy agreed. She decided to go back to the burned house early the next morning. Bess could not go with her, but George was free to drive out to the Allison property.

By nine o'clock the two girls were on their way. En route Nancy explained everything that had happened the night before.

"I've been thinking it over and can't help but believe that Mrs. Allison told the truth last night," Nancy said. "Or at least she feels sure that Rishi is hidden at the burned house.

"It occurred to me that the police may have missed the branch-off of the tunnel. That's why I'm going back there."

When the girls reached the Allison property, Nancy hid the car in a clump of trees and, as before, the girls walked the remaining distance. They were moving along the path when George caught her friend's hand.

"Someone is coming!" she whispered.

The girls dodged back among the bushes just as Jasper Batt strode into view. He carried a small package in his hand and a Thermos protruded from a coat pocket. Nancy and George waited until he had disappeared before they emerged from their hiding place.

"I have a hunch that Mr. Batt is taking breakfast to someone," Nancy said. "Let's follow. He may lead us to Rishi and Rai!"

As the girls cautiously trailed the man, who finally went uphill, it became evident he was heading for the rock door. They saw him pause by the secret entrance.

"How does he intend to enter?" Nancy whispered. "Watch closely."

The man picked up a heavy stick from the ground and rapped six times in succession on the rock door. He waited several minutes, then repeated the raps.

The girls heard a faint click. Jasper Batt stepped back a pace, waiting expectantly. The massive door slowly swung outward. Batt thrust the package of food and the Thermos into the tunnel.

Nancy and George heard him speak a few words to someone inside, but the girls were too far away to distinguish what they were. After a moment Batt firmly closed the rock door, then walked off swiftly into the woods.

"He probably brought food to a prisoner in the tunnel," George whispered.

"Rishi!" Nancy added. "I'll find out! I'll try Jasper Batt's trick of opening the door."

"But maybe Rai's inside, too. He might harm you!" George warned.

But the girl detective, who was less concerned about her own safety than Rishi's, moved forward. Using the same heavy stick that Batt had dropped nearby, Nancy rapped sharply six times. She waited expectantly, but nothing happened.

"Batt repeated the signals," George reminded her.

Again Nancy knocked on the door. This time the girls heard the familiar click of the latch. They moved back, making room for the heavy barrier to swing outward. Nancy and George peered into the dark interior of the tunnel.

"I can't see a thing," George whispered.

"Rishi! Rishi!" Nancy cried out.

"Help! Help!" came a feeble voice.

Nancy and George knew that it was not Rishi who had answered. The voice sounded familiar, but they could not place it.

"Who are you and where are you?" Nancy shouted.

"Putnam—Peter Putnam! Batt has me chained to a post! Come over and free me!"

"It may be a trap," George warned Nancy.

The young detective shook her head. By this time her eyes had grown accustomed to the dark cavern and she could dimly make out a figure chained to a post a few feet from the entrance. The heavy metal was locked to his wrists and ankles; the chains were long enough for him to reach the door but not to escape. Nancy entered the tunnel with George following.

"Thank goodness you've come in time!" Putnam murmured brokenly. "Those men wanted me to die in this dark, filthy hole."

"Why?" Nancy asked him.

Peter Putnam rattled his chains angrily. "Get me out of here!"

"I'll be glad to after you tell me where Rishi is."

"Why should I tell you anything?" the prisoner growled. "You stole the papers from my coffeepot!"

"The documents weren't yours," Nancy said. "Right now it's in your interest to tell me everything you know about Rai and Rishi. Unless you do, I may be compelled to leave you here."

Although she had no intention of abandoning the man, Nancy turned as if to depart. Her move brought a quick response.

"All right, I'll tell you everything I know," Putnam replied. "But first, unfasten these chains!"

"I prefer to hear your story first," Nancy insisted. "Where has Rishi been hidden?"

"Rai has him at my place—a prisoner in the loft. I was to get a nice sum for keeping my mouth shut about it. But this is the pay I get! Chained to a post! If you don't believe me I'll take you there and prove it!"

"That's exactly what I want you to do!" Nancy said.

Nancy and George set to work with a huge rock to break the lock of the chain. Together they finally succeeded. Putnam crept to the tunnel entrance, whimpering from pain as circulation returned to his cramped limbs.

"You'll be all right in a few minutes," Nancy encouraged him. "Lean on my shoulder and I'll help you to the car."

"What will you do when you get to my place?" Putnam asked. "That fellow Rai is a cunning fox. You'll be no match for him."

"You must help us, Mr. Putnam."

The man said nothing and Nancy, casting a quick glance in his direction, guessed he had no intention of aiding anyone but himself.

Presently Nancy pulled up a little distance from Putnam's barnlike home and stopped the car. She did not want the running of the engine to warn Rai that someone was approaching the house.

"You can sneak up to the house the back way," Putnam suggested, indicating a path that led through the underbrush. "I'll wait there," he added, as the three got out of the car.

Nancy and George looked at the man with ill-concealed contempt but said nothing. They crept alone toward the house.

After circling it, Nancy quietly twisted the knob and pushed the door open a tiny crack.

"The coast is clear, I think," she whispered. "I can't hear a sound."

Nancy opened the door wider and the two girls entered on tiptoe. A harsh laugh caused them to wheel about. Rai! He slammed the door shut and faced them, gloating.

"So! I now have two fair prisoners to enclose in my little cage!"

Instantly Nancy and George sprang at the man, hoping to overpower him and regain their freedom before he could grab them. Although they fought with all their strength, and George used her knowledge of Judo, Rai merely laughed at their efforts. He held them off as if they were puppets. Then he caught up a piece of rope from the kitchen table and trussed the girls securely.

They eyed Rai silently, wondering what punishment he might inflict on them. In all their experience with criminals they had never encountered a man with such strength.

"What have you done with Rishi!" Nancy gasped, recovering her poise.

"Ah! So that is why you come? Rishi is dead."

"I do not believe you," Nancy cried out. "You have him hidden in the loft."

As if to confirm her words, the girls heard a slight noise overhead. Rai smiled blandly.

"You are correct. Rishi lives, but his hours are numbered. He knows too much. He must die that Iama Togara may live in peace. Next we will find his father and put him to sleep."

"You don't realize what you're saying, Rai," Nancy said pleadingly. "The boy has never done you any harm. Let him go free."

"No, it is decreed that Rishi must die by my hand. He shall die slowly and in a manner befitting a maharaja."

Turning his back upon the two girls, Rai moved toward the ladder leading to the loft.

CHAPTER XX

The Secret of the Charm

"WAIT!" Nancy cried frantically. "Rai, you must be out of your mind even to think of such horrible deeds. Don't you realize that if you harm Rishi the authorities will punish you, maybe even by death."

The man paused, his foot on the lowest rung of the ladder.

"Rai is safe from all harm," he said. "The ivory charm bestows absolute protection. It is now in my possession."

"So it was you who stole the lucky piece from me at the fraternity house," said Nancy. "I suspected it was you."

Rai laughed gloatingly as he significantly tapped his chest to indicate that he wore the charm hidden beneath his shirt.

"Not only does my charm bring good luck to

the wearer but it has the power of life and death!" he added dramatically.

"What do you mean by that?" Nancy asked anxiously.

Again the man laughed softly, and said, "There are many mysteries that may never be revealed."

"You are hopelessly superstitious if you believe the charm will protect you from the police," George spoke up, sparring for time. "Mrs. Allison already has been arrested."

The girls knew from the change of expression on Rai's face that he had not heard this piece of news before.

He recovered quickly and said calmly, "My duty does not change. Rishi must die!"

Both Nancy and George continued to plead in vain with Rai, but he paid no attention. Muttering angrily, he mounted the ladder and vanished into the loft.

"We must do something!" Nancy told George, tugging at her ropes. "We can't let Rai commit this dreadful crime!"

Both girls worked at their bonds until their wrists were cut and bleeding. It was impossible to loosen the ropes.

Overhead they could hear Rai muttering in a singsong voice. Apparently he was intoning a weird incantation over Rishi. They could distinguish moans from the boy, and knew that he must be suffering intensely. Then all became quiet.

"Ah!" they heard Rai cry out in triumph. "Rishi enters the eternal sleep from which there is no awakening. Only the ivory charm can save him now—and I have it." He gave a cruel laugh.

"Did you hear what he said?" Nancy whispered to George. "The charm! If only we could get it, we might still save poor Rishi!"

"The charm would bring him back to consciousness," Nancy said, thinking aloud. "I am sure of it. For a long while I have suspected the truth—now I am certain of it. The ivory charm guards the secret of life and death!"

"Do you realize what you are saying?" George gasped.

"Yes! It all comes back to me now—what Dr. Stackpole told me about the life-giving fluid sometimes found in the hidden cavities of ancient Indian charms!"

"Nancy, I don't know what you mean."

She quickly explained, then said, "We must try to get that piece, George. It is our only hope of saving Rishi."

"If we can ever untie these knots," George started to say but did not finish.

Nancy would not give up. The girl detective and her friend strained and tugged until they were exhausted. Tears of disappointment came to their eyes. They tried not to think of Rishi in the loft above.

"Listen!" George whispered suddenly. "I hear a car coming!"

"Perhaps Peter Putnam has brought help!" Nancy said.

George commanded a view of the window. A moment later she whispered excitedly that she could see several men stealing toward the house.

"They may be detectives, Nancy. Let's take a chance and call for help."

"Wait until they're at the door," Nancy cautioned. "Then all escape will be cut off for Rai."

A minute later, when the men were nearby, the girls raised their voices together. Alarmed by their cries, Rai scrambled down from the loft. Just then the men burst inside and announced they were police detectives.

"Arrest this man!" Nancy cried.

The animal trainer made a dive for the nearest window but was caught roughly by the shoulder and hauled back, handcuffed, and led away. Other detectives quickly set Nancy and George free.

"Rishi is upstairs in the loft," Nancy told the detectives, as her ropes were being severed. "Rai says he's dead, but maybe he's not! Oh, I hope he's not!"

On a sudden inspiration she asked a policeman to take the ivory charm from Rai's neck and give it to her.

"This may help," she said.

At that very moment Bess Marvin rushed into the room followed by a man.

"Mr. Tilak!" Nancy cried. "Here is the ivory charm from your family. Does it have any magical powers?"

"Yes," he replied. "It contains a special antidote against various harmful drugs."

"Then follow me," she directed, and scooted up the ladder.

Puzzled, he and Bess followed quickly. George arrived a moment later. A discouraging sight met their eyes. Rishi lay on the floor, colorless and limp. An officer was giving him mouth-to-mouth resuscitation, with no noticeable result.

"Mr. Tilak," said Nancy, handing him the ivory charm, "this is your son Rishi. Please use the restorative quickly!"

The former maharaja was trembling with emotion as he gazed at the boy, but he took the charm and kneeled beside the young victim.

"Hold my boy's mouth open," he quietly said to Nancy.

When she did, Mr. Tilak deftly broke off one of the elephant's feet and poured the fluid it contained under Rishi's tongue. Everyone waited with bated breath for some response from the boy.

Nancy could see Mr. Tilak's lips moving as if in prayer. A few seconds later Rishi began to breathe.

"He lives!" his father exclaimed.

"He lives!" murmured everyone in the loft with a private prayer of thanks.

There was silence for several seconds, until the watchers were sure of this. When Rishi opened his eyes, the policemen quietly left the loft.

The young Indian boy looked at Nancy, Bess, George, and the strange man beside him.

"How do you feel?" Nancy asked.

"Rishi fine now," he replied weakly. "Rai gone."

"I have some wonderful news for you," Nancy said. "Rai is in jail and can never harm you again. And Rishi, this man is your father, who thought you had died as a baby."

Father and son gazed at each other, too overcome to speak. Nancy gave a signal to Bess and George that they should all go downstairs quietly and leave the two alone.

When the girls reached the first floor, Bess burst out, "Isn't it wonderful. Just think, Nancy, you found Rishi's father for him!"

Nancy smiled and asked, "Bess, how did you happen to come here and bring Mr. Tilak?"

Bess explained that when she finished her errands, she had stopped at Nancy's house.

"Hannah told me where you had gone. Also Mr. Tilak phoned. On the spur of the moment I asked him if he'd like to come with me to meet you. While passing this place, I saw a lot of cars—policemen's and yours, Nancy. So I drove in."

"You certainly came at the right moment," Nancy said.

George spoke. "Nancy, if Mr. Tilak hadn't arrived to break open the elephant charm, would you have done it?"

"Yes, to save Rishi's life. I admit I had a hunch it held some form of restorative," she replied.

In a few minutes Rishi and his father descended the ladder. The boy had completely recovered and the two were smiling broadly.

Mr. Tilak held the beautiful ivory charm.

"Nancy," he said, "Rishi and I can never repay you for what you have done for us. But as a token of our appreciation, we will have this ivory charm repaired, then present it to you as our most precious material object."

"Oh, I don't want to take such a priceless treasure from you," she said quickly.

"We insist," Mr. Tilak replied. "Rishi tells me you also recovered our stolen fortune in jewels. You and your friends who helped you shall have mementos from that collection, too."

Nancy was embarrassed and quickly told him she never solved mysteries for anything but the sheer delight of it. Her mind wandered a moment as she hoped another mystery would come her way soon. It turned out to be an exciting adventure about *The Whispering Statue*.

George suddenly grinned. "Mr. Tilak, before you repair the ivory charm for Nancy you'd better put a powerful restorative inside. She always has close calls when she solves a mystery!"

Everyone laughed and agreed the idea was a good one.